Lucas had been wanting to kiss Sherri for months.

Tonight, he finally gave in to his natural desire. He leaned his head close to hers. He took his time, savoring the first touch of her soft, inviting mouth. The light pressure was followed by his tongue tenderly outlining the curve of her lips, teasing them open to receive him. She responded by parting her lips, opening wide enough to take his tongue against her own, permitting him to give her the pleasure she'd previously denied herself. Their mouths mated like lovers who'd been away from each other for too long.

His hands cupped her face. She stroked his shoulders, sliding up to his neck. Holding him gently but firmly, she allowed the kiss to deepen while their tongues did an extended, sensual dance, stroking and tasting until it seemed as though they had done this many, many times. It could have gone on for minutes or hours—Lucas didn't know and he didn't care. All he knew at that moment was that he didn't want this kiss to end.

Books by Melanie Schuster

Harlequin Kimani Romance

Working Man
Model Perfect Passion
Trust in Me
A Case for Romance
Picture Perfect Christmas
Chemistry of Desire
Poetry Man
Way to Her Heart

MELANIE SCHUSTER

started reading when she was four. Currently, it is still a passion, and whenever she has a spare moment she is reading. Fascinated with books and the art of story-telling, she wanted to be a writer from the time she was very young. She fell in love with romances when she began reading the books her mother brought home. As she grew older, she would go to any store that sold paperbacks and load up on her own.

Melanie loves romances because they are always hopeful. Despite the harsh realities of life, romance always brings to mind the wonderful, exciting adventure of falling in love with a soul mate. She believes in love and romance with all her heart, and she finds fulfillment in writing stories about compelling couples who find true, lasting love in the face of obstacles. She hopes all her readers find their true love. If they've already been lucky enough to find love, she hopes that they never forget what it felt like to fall in love.

Way to her heart

Melanie Schuster

HARLEQUIN® KIMANI™ ROMANCE

To Virgie Tiyen Wilson,
for all the things she does. You're my calm in the storm,
my idea person, my reader and my friend.

To my dear aunts, Pauline Ragland,
an exceptional example of what a real woman is
all about, and Theresa Cole, who taught me many things
by example, especially how to be a wonderful aunt!
Thanks for all the special memories.

ISBN-13: 978-0-373-86297-9

WAY TO HER HEART

Copyright © 2013 by Melanie Schuster

Recycling programs
for this product may
not exist in your area.

Printed in U.S.A.

www.Harlequin.com

Dear Reader,

Thanks for coming on another trip to Columbia, South Carolina, for more love and excitement. This time it was Dr. Sherri Stratton's turn to find her love, with Lucas VanBuren, thanks to her very sweet and precocious daughter Sydney.

Those of you who live in the south know all about the Spoleto Festival that Lucas and Sherri visit. If you've never been, you should go—it's amazing!

The farmer's market in the Honey Horn area of Hilton Head is also a real place. I do love a farmer's market. Or any upscale market where you can buy exotic goods as well as local produce. I do love to cook, so writing about the VanBuren chefs is a lot of fun for me, and I hope all my foodie readers are enjoying it, too.

Until next time, keep reading and stay blessed!

Melanie

I Chronicles 4:10

melanieschuster@sbcglobal.net

Thanks to all my readers who have also become my friends. I couldn't do this without your enthusiastic support and encouragement.

Prologue

It was the best wedding she'd ever been to in her entire life. Since Sydney Stratton was just six going on seven years old, she hadn't been to very many, but this one was absolutely wonderful. Her mommy's best friend, Auntie Alexis, had married Jared VanBuren and Sydney was a flower girl, a responsibility she took seriously. She and Courtney, the other flower girl, got to wear beautiful dresses and carry pretty baskets full of rose petals that they sprinkled on the white runner. They had their hair done in Alexis's spa, and they even got to wear nail polish to match the red lace appliqués on their dresses and the red wreaths of rosebuds in their hair. After the wedding they had the honor of walking Alexis's little dogs at the reception, and it was a lot of fun.

Marriage was a pretty awesome thing from what Sydney could see. Her mommy's other best friend, Auntie Emily, was the first of them to get married. She had married a really nice man named Todd. He was a doctor and he was tall and handsome and Auntie Emily smiled all the time now. She and Todd had two babies, twin boys, which Sydney thought was just wonderful. Auntie Alexis's new husband was handsome, too, and he was a chef, an important chef who'd been on TV. He gave Alexis the nicest things, especially Sookie and Honeybee, two cute little Welsh Corgi puppies.

He also had a lot of family, including twin brothers named Lucas and Damon. They were both very nice, but Lucas was especially nice because he knew how much Sydney liked to try different foods. He always had something special for her to taste at the new restaurant he and Jared owned. He liked to laugh and he could do magic tricks. He could dance really well, too. He had danced with her mother all night at the reception. He always made pretty eyes at her mother, Sherri. He looked at her a lot and he was always smiling when he did. He also made her laugh a lot, which was very good. Sydney's mother was a busy doctor and she needed someone around to help her relax and have fun, even though Sydney did those things pretty well, too.

Sydney was having a good time at the reception, playing with Courtney and making sure that Sookie and Honeybee behaved themselves. Lucas came over to their table with his twin brother, Damon, and he did another trick for them before he asked Damon to watch the little dogs while he danced with Sydney. He took her out on the dance floor and they danced with great gusto until the music changed. When it slowed down, he had her stand on his feet while they danced to the slow music. It was so much fun that she couldn't stop smiling. This was definitely the most fun she'd ever had and she didn't want it to end. After the music stopped, Lucas picked her up and swung her around in his strong arms before giving her a big kiss on the cheek.

"Let's see what your mom is up to, shall we?"

As they walked through the crowd to the table where her mommy was laughing and talking with the other bridesmaids, Sydney got a brilliant idea. She was a smart little girl and she was always thinking, but she'd never had an idea that was this wonderful. She decided that her mommy was going to get married next—to Lucas. Then they could have a wonderful time forever. All she had to do was make a really good plan and everything would work out perfectly.

Chapter 1

Sherri Stratton yawned as she stretched lazily on the comfortable chaise lounge. "This is the best Mother's Day I've had since the day Sydney was born," she said with a happy little sigh.

She was relaxing on the deck of the new home of the VanBurens, the in-laws of her BFF, Alexis Sharp VanBuren. Alexis was next to her on another chaise and she agreed wholeheartedly. "I'm not a mom yet, but it's not for lacking of trying. I still can't believe that the VanBuren men thought up this weekend of pampering all by themselves, but if this is the treatment I can look forward to as a mommy, I can't wait to have a baby of my own."

"There's no rush, is there? You and Jared have only

been married since February and you're already trying for a little one?" Sherri adjusted the sunny yellow tank top that matched the bright floral shorts and reached for the iced tea that was on a small table between the two chaises.

Alexis took a sip of tea before answering. "I'm not racing to the maternity ward or anything, but we both want children. And, honey, the process of baby making is so much fun that it's a win-win situation for me," she said with a sexy laugh.

Sherri almost choked on her sweet tea as she sat up and lifted her oversize sunglasses to stare at her friend. "Alexis! You act like we're alone out here. Too much information, girl."

Her new mother-in-law, Vanessa Lomax VanBuren, was also on the deck with Vanessa's mother, Delilah Peters, and Alexis's mother, Aretha Sharp. All the women laughed at Sherri's embarrassment.

"Remember, I'm married to Jared's father so I know what she's talking about. How do you think I ended up with all those children?" Vanessa's smile was identical to the one on Alexis's face. Vanessa's mother, Delilah, chimed in.

"There's nothing wrong with appreciating the romantic aspects of marriage. It's been a long time since Vanessa's father passed away, but I have a lifetime of wonderful memories to recall," she said.

Sherri's face was still pink when Aretha had her say. "Sherri, darlin', you're a doctor. A pediatrician, at that.

You know how babies get here, and you're blushing like a schoolgirl. You know what I think?"

Alexis rolled her eyes as she took another sip of tea. "I'm sure you're going to tell us, Mama. It's not like you can keep anything to yourself."

Aretha ignored her daughter's little barb and kept on rolling. "I think that it's way past time for you to get married. Or at least take a lover. You haven't dated anyone since Sydney was born, and she's about to turn seven. You're beautiful, smart, accomplished and it's a crying shame that you're keeping all that wonderfulness to yourself. What in the world are you waiting for?"

A healthy spray of tea from her mouth was Sherri's reaction to Aretha's remark. She was closer to Aretha than to her own mother and she was used to the older woman speaking her mind on any and every topic, but she was surprised by her frankness in front of the other ladies. They didn't seem to think anything was amiss. Delilah was more than happy to join in the conversation.

"You don't have a young man? Honey, that doesn't make any sense at all. Do you prefer women, dear? I'm not judging—I'm just curious," she admitted.

"Mother! That's rather personal, don't you think?" Vanessa shook her head as she chided her outspoken mother.

Aretha and Alexis were trying hard not to laugh while Sherri blotted the tea off her face and chest. She was totally accustomed to being around older women who spoke their minds, so she wasn't insulted, but she did feel the need to explain herself.

"Well, Ms. Delilah, it's not that I prefer the company of women or anything like that. It's just that being a single mother is something I take very seriously. I made a decision not to date until Sydney is out of high school. I don't think it's a good idea to have a bunch of random men parading in and out of her life."

Delilah raised a delicately arched eyebrow. "Well, honey, nobody wants you to be a hoochie. There's no need for a whole parade. If you get the right soloist, you'll have all the music you need," she said with a wicked grin.

Sherri had to laugh. Ms. Delilah had a point, even if it didn't really apply to Sherri's situation.

The sounds of laughter floated into the kitchen, where Lucas VanBuren was making more iced tea for the ladies while Sydney, his self-appointed sous chef, was seated at the work island arranging his freshly baked tea cakes in a flat wicker basket lined with a big cloth napkin. She looked completely absorbed in her task, but her mind was focused on something else. She looked just like her mother; she was tall for her age, slender and fair-skinned with a light dusting of freckles across her nose. Her hair was the same reddish-brown as her mother's, but unlike Sherri's, it wasn't in a short, fashionable bob. Sydney wore her hair parted in the middle with two long braids that were currently covered with a bandanna so she could look like Lucas, her idol. Her round glasses didn't disguise her big, bright eyes; they just made her look even cuter.

As she carefully placed the last tea cake in the basket, she dusted the light coating of sugar off her fingertips and looked intently at Lucas. He was so tall and so handsome that it was easy to overlook the things she really liked about him. He was funny and nice and kind and he was the best cook in the world, even better than his brother Jared, in Sydney's opinion. She'd had several months to observe him, and she was more convinced than ever that he'd be the perfect husband for her mother. Now was the perfect time to launch her plan.

"Uncle Lucas, do you like my mommy?" she asked innocently.

He smiled down at her as he stirred simple syrup into the tea. "Of course I do, sweetie. I like you, too."

Sydney smiled back, flashing her deep dimples. "I like you, too. A whole lot," she confided. "But do you really, really like my mommy?"

Lucas finished stirring the tea and added slices of lemons and pineapple to the pitcher. He sat on the stool next to Sydney and crossed his arms as he met her intelligent gaze.

"Yes, I really, really like your mommy. She's very pretty and smart and she has a lovely personality. Why are you so curious about this all of a sudden?"

Sydney crossed her legs and linked her hands around one knee. "Because I think you should marry her."

A year ago, even six months ago, Lucas would have had a different reaction to her words. He was far too busy dating a wide variety of women to even think about settling down with one. Many ladies had tried and failed to slip a matrimonial noose around his neck, and he had evaded them all with ease. But that had all changed when his brother married Alexis and Lucas met Dr. Sherri Stratton. The first time he saw her smile, he was captured. Her smooth skin, those dimples, and the intelligence and humor that sparkled in her eyes all got to him in an instant. When he finally got around to observing the rest of her, he was even more impressed. Sherri was brainy and accomplished, in addition to being a real beauty.

In his younger years the brains and accomplishments wouldn't have meant as much as the fact that she was a certified dime piece, but now they did. However, one of the things that made Sherri superlative in Lucas's eyes was sitting next to him with her eyes locked on his. Anyone who could raise a child as sweet and engaging as Sydney had to be an amazing person.

"So are you going to do it, Uncle Lucas?"

He had to focus quickly in order to give her an intelligent response. "Why do you think I should marry your mom, sweetie?"

"Because she should have a really nice husband like Uncle Todd and Uncle Jared. She should have someone to be sweet to her. My auntie Emily is really happy now that she has Uncle Todd, and Auntie Alexis is really happy with Uncle Jared, and I want my mommy to be happy, too."

Lucas was bemused by her astute analysis of the situation. "Why do you think I'd make her happy?"

Sydney pushed her glasses up and started counting off reasons on her fingers. "Because you're very nice. You talk to everybody and you treat everybody like they're important. You make her laugh. You're very handsome, but that's just a bonus. You have a nice family and they like me. And you're very nice to me."

"You've given this a lot of thought, Sydney. Are you sure I'm the right guy? You realize that if I was to marry your mom I'd be your stepfather," he said carefully. "Did you think about that?"

"Of course I did. I think you'd be good at it. Do you think I'd be a good little girl to have around?"

"You'd be the best in the world, sweetie. But what would your own daddy think about someone else in your life?" he asked gently.

"I don't think he thinks about me at all," she replied with a shrug. "I've never met him. He and my mommy weren't married and he went away when he found out about me."

Lucas felt his throat tighten at the idea of a man walking away from a woman like Sherri and ignoring an adorable child like Sydney. He'd often wondered if Sherri was divorced or widowed—because there clearly was no husband in the current picture—but he'd never asked Alexis about her marital status. Alexis was his sister-in-law, but he figured she wouldn't appreciate being interrogated about her best friend. He didn't have a chance to dwell on the information he'd just received because Sydney wanted an answer. Right now.

"So are you going to do it, Uncle Lucas?"

She was totally serious—Lucas could see that. He wasn't about to promise her something he couldn't deliver, but he was totally on board with the idea. He'd asked Sherri out a few times, and so far she'd turned him down.

"It's not just up to me, darlin'. What makes you think your mommy likes me? I might not be her type. What kind of guys does she usually date?" Wow, that was kind of sleazy. It was just wrong of him to use this situation to pump a six-year-old for information about her mother. But Sydney didn't see it like that at all.

"She doesn't go out, Uncle Lucas. Not with guys. She takes care of me and she takes care of her patients and we go to church and we visit with people and we have picnics and things, but she doesn't have boyfriends."

"Well, maybe she doesn't want one. Have you thought about that? Maybe she's happy with her life the way it is."

Sydney nodded her head. "She says that all the time when Aunt Emily and Aunt Alexis try to get her to go on a date. She says she's happy and she's not going out with anybody until I'm in high school. That's a long time, Uncle Lucas! I don't think she should wait that long, do you?"

The word *no* came out of his mouth before he could stop it. No, he surely didn't think that Sherri should deny herself the pleasure of having a mate for years to come. "I can see that this means a lot to you, and you're really sweet to think about your mommy's happiness, but I can't just walk up to her and ask her to marry me," he said.

"No, you can't. That's why you have to start slow. You have to take baby steps first, Uncle Lucas."

She sounded so wise and worldly that Lucas had to smother a laugh. "Sydney, you're pretty sure of yourself. This is a big enterprise you're talking about. I like your mom a lot, but it's going to take more than that for the two of us to start dating. I think this is something that you need to leave up to your mom. It has to be her decision, and you and I have to respect her wishes."

"Uncle Lucas, don't be a chicken baby. No pain, no gain, no gain, no glory."

"Where in the world did you get that from?"

Sydney looked thoughtful as she told him she'd heard it on the Food Network. "I was watching Iron Chef America and Alton Brown said it. It made sense to me."

This time Lucas laughed out loud. "Sydney, are you sure you're only six? That's some mighty grown-up thinking for a little girl."

"I'll be seven in a little while. And I'm precocious— my teacher said so. So, what are you going to do first? We have to have a plan. If you fail to plan, you plan to fail. That's on Mommy's quote-of-the-day calendar," she informed him.

"The first thing we need to do is take these refreshments to the ladies. Next I need to go to the store for some more provisions. Do you want to come with me?"

Her face lit up and she agreed. "That's a good idea. We can make our plans on the way."

He scooped her up off the high stool and placed her on the floor. Lucas covered the basket of tea cakes with another cloth napkin and handed it to Sydney along with a stack of smaller napkins. After filling a clear ice bucket, he grabbed the pitcher of tea and they went out on the deck to replenish the drinks. They were greeted with joy when the plump, golden pastries were revealed. Sydney took her job as server quite seriously, making sure that each woman had a fresh napkin and a fragrant, vanilla-scented cake. Lucas refilled each glass with fresh ice and sweet tea, making sure that everyone was comfortable as he did so. He was complimentary and attentive to all the ladies, but he had a private remark for Sherri. He refilled her glass and handed it to her with a smile.

"Sherri, as you know, we're making a special Mother's Day dinner today and I need to go to the market for a few things. Would it be okay if Sydney went with me? We won't be gone very long."

Sherri slipped her sunglasses off and gave him the brilliant smile that never failed to warm his heart. "Sure, if you promise not to let her talk you into buying crazy things. Everything she sees on the Food Network she wants to try, so watch out or you'll end up with a basket full of durian fruit and oxtails, or something equally odd."

Lucas gave her a smile of pleasure. Not many people could reference the famously smelly tropical fruit like that. It was just one more thing he liked about her—the fact that she knew about food. He was about to answer her when his grandmother spoke up.

Delilah looked at her grandson and then at Sherri. "Now this is what I was talking about. Sherri, you and Lucas make a lovely couple. He's a perfect choice for you," she said warmly.

Sherri's eyes grew wide but before she could get really embarrassed, Jared and his father returned from walking the dogs on the beach. There were four pups; two belonged to the elder VanBurens and two belonged to Alexis and Jared. Lucas took advantage of the happy commotion created by the dogs to suggest that Sherri should make her escape.

"Hey, if you want to hide out, come with us to the market. My gran means no harm but she has no problem getting into other people's business," he said with a rueful grin.

"You know what? That sounds like a great idea," Sherri agreed, and in minutes they'd made their getaway.

Chapter 2

Sherri was surprised at how much she enjoyed her excursion with Lucas. Sydney was supposed to go with them, but she opted to stay and play with the dogs. She doted on the energetic little Corgis and Sherri had no doubt that there was going to be a puppy or two in their very near future. So that left her all alone with Lucas. It wasn't awkward or uncomfortable at all because she was used to him. Ever since her bestie Alexis had married Jared VanBuren, the members of his family had become fairly familiar to Sherri.

She and Lucas had been partners in the wedding and he'd been a lot of fun. He was a good dancer and a great conversationalist. Since he'd moved to Columbia to take over as executive chef at Seven-Seventeen, the restaurant owned by the VanBuren brothers, she saw him fairly often. Lucas was a swell guy, no doubt about it. He was also quite good-looking. He was a perfect combination of his African-American mother and Caucasian father, with thick, wavy, golden-brown hair, green eyes and tawny skin. He was nice and tall, too; all the VanBuren men were inches over six feet.

"Is there something in my teeth? Do I have a hanger or something?" He flipped down the visor to peer in the mirror and stare in his nostrils with mock anxiety.

"No, you don't. I'd tell you if you did, promise," Sherri said with a laugh.

"You're staring at me. I thought I looked weird or something."

"Not at all. I was just thinking about how good-looking you are. Your whole family, I mean. You Van-Burens are a handsome crew," she said.

"Thanks, but I can't take credit for that. I merely reap the benefits of a beautiful mixture of races and genes. My mom and dad are the ones who have the good looks. They were just kind enough to share them with us. Just like you shared yours with Sydney. She looks just like you," he said. He had a deep, rich voice and she enjoyed listening to him talk.

"Our baby pictures are identical," she confessed.

"Okay, here's the place," Lucas said as he turned into the parking lot of the giant farmers' market located on a part of Hilton Head island known as Honey Horn.

Sherri was duly impressed with the huge, immaculately kept facility. She was so busy looking at the market that she almost missed the fact that Lucas had opened her car door. She put her hand into his absently until she felt the warmth of his strong fingers. A sensation like a mild electric shock raced right up her arm, spreading warmth as it went. *Wow. What was that?* Profoundly glad that Lucas had glanced at something in the distance, Sherri gracefully exited the car. She was pretty sure she had a goofy expression on her face and she was relieved he hadn't seen it. Luckily, he didn't seem to have noticed her momentary schoolgirl foolishness. As they entered the market, Sherri inhaled the fresh smells of the gorgeous produce displayed in tempting piles.

"Sydney would love this. She might have forsaken her beloved doggies to see all of this."

They stopped by a stand that sold locally made baskets. Lucas bought two large ones and a T-shirt with the market logo for Sydney. "Now she won't feel like she missed out. We'll have to bring her here the next time we're on the island."

"That's so thoughtful of you," Sherri said warmly. "She's a big fan of yours. She thinks you're the funniest man she ever met and she says that you cook better than Jared, and that's high praise because she knows her food."

"You have an amazing kid, Sherri. Smart, well-behaved, cute as a button and a budding gourmet. You're a great mom."

Sherri stopped looking at the heirloom tomatoes in unusual colors and gave him a big smile. "Thank you for saying that. My life is all about Sydney and my job. I had just started my internship when I found out I was pregnant. It wasn't easy, but it sure was worth it. She's the best thing that ever happened to me."

"I hope her father feels the same way about her."

Only someone who knew her really well would have been able to read the look on her face, fleeting though it was. She was about to give him an answer when her cell phone rang. Grateful for the distraction, she hastily answered it. It was Alexis, being her usual nosy self.

"I was just checking on you," she said cheerfully. "You two got out of here so fast I didn't realize you were gone. Having fun?"

"Yes, I am. Is my daughter behaving?"

"She's always a perfect little lady, you know that. I'm going to let you change the subject because you get that weird look on your face when you don't want to talk about something and I don't want Lucas to think you're nuts. So you're safe for now."

"You're too kind," Sherri mumbled.

Alexis ignored her snarky reply and went on. "My darling husband wants his brother to bring home more lemons and shallots and some fresh basil along with whatever else he went to get. And he says he's making the fire now so it'll be hot when you two get back."

"I'll let him know. We should be back soon."

"Good because while they're grilling dinner, I'm gonna be grilling you!"

Sherri ended the call while Alexis was still giggling madly. As she put the phone back in the pocket of her shorts, Lucas returned to her side. She relayed Jared's requests and he nodded absently. Taking her hand, he began to lead her to the aisle where the shallots and other aromatics were. He looked down at her with a warm look of concern.

"Is everything okay? You had kind of an odd look when you were on the phone," he said.

"It's a bad habit," she admitted. "I make the strangest faces without realizing it. I don't do it at work—just when Alexis is picking on me."

"You two are as close as sisters and if you're anything like my family, y'all probably pick on each other constantly. Besides, it's cute as hell when you do it."

He squeezed her hand and gave her another of his crooked smiles. The same warm thrill ran through her as before, making her forget about the teasing she'd endured earlier and the interrogation she was sure to face once Alexis got her alone. For once, she was in the moment, just enjoying Lucas's company.

As far as Lucas was concerned the weekend was a total success. He got to take the baby steps that Sydney had advised simply by taking Sherri to the farmers' market. They had some time alone and he got to look at her long, shapely legs as much as he wanted. Everything about her appealed to him, from her thick, coarse hair with its stylish cut, to her sweet, natural face with the sprinkling of tiny freckles across her nose. She was graceful and sexy without making a big deal of it. He was used to artificially pretty women who made a big deal of their beauty like it was a new kind of currency. The message they sent out was "I'm irresistible because I have long hair and big boobs, so have sex with me!" Lucas was no snob and he had a very high sex drive besides, so their willingness to engage in frisky sex was very convenient for much of his dating life, but not anymore. Now it was annoying to Lucas. It was easy enough to get what he wanted from the bouncy-boobie-bunny kind of woman, but he no longer desired that kind of relationship. It was like eating in five-star restaurants after a lifetime of fast food; now that he knew better, he did better.

Sherri was a different kind of woman altogether. She was a challenge. Besides being fresh, pretty and accomplished, she was a mother with a very smart and charming child. There was no margin for error here. He had to come correct or not come at all. When kids were involved, all other bets were off. He couldn't just hop aboard Sherri for some fun-filled sex and go on his merry way—not that he wanted to. He had a strong desire for her—that much was true. But he wanted way more than sex. Sex was a wonderful thing and he looked forward to having lots of it with Sherri, but that was just the beginning of what he wanted to share with her.

He had sat across from her at the dinner table just to watch her eat. Everyone raved about the food and ate with great appetites, but the way Sherri consumed her meal was extremely enticing. He and Jared had made a real feast, starting with goat cheese crostini and a platter of marinated vegetables fresh from the market. The way she looked eating the spears of asparagus and cucumber was stimulating to say the least. The entrée consisted of grilled lobster and jumbo shrimp, with tender breasts of chicken and petite filet mignons. This was accompanied by dainty grilled pattypan squash, colorful fingerling potatoes and long, crisp *haricots verts* with cremini mushrooms. When he wasn't watching the sensual way Sherri enjoyed the meal, he was keeping an eye on Sydney. She had excellent table manners and an equally good appetite. She ate everything on her plate and came back for more of her favorites, the pickled golden beets and the squash.

After the sumptuous meal, everyone had decided to wait a while before having dessert. The men cleaned up the kitchen and the women walked off their meal on the beach while the dogs got a nice run. With all the inquiring minds away from the house, Jared decided it was a great time to get in his younger brother's business.

"You were all but drooling on Sherri, bro. What's going on there?"

Lucas didn't take offense; he just shrugged. "Nothing's going on yet. I've asked her out a couple of times and she's been busy, but I think that's about to change.

I'm ninety percent sure that the next time I ask, she'll say yes."

Jared raised an eyebrow and said, "That's all well and good, but don't be fooling around. In case you haven't noticed, she's not your typical empty-headed glamazon. And she has a child, a very smart and lovable child, so you can't be treating her place like it's got a revolving door on it."

"Don't hold back, Jared. Tell me how you really feel," Lucas said dryly. "I'm not an idiot. I know exactly what kind of lady Sherri is and I have nothing but respect for her. And love for her daughter, if you must know. Sydney's an amazing kid. I'd never do anything to hurt her."

Jared opened his mouth for a comment, but his father spoke first. "Glad to hear you say that, son. Dr. Sherri Stratton seems like a lovely woman and she's certainly raised an exceptional child. Go slowly and carefully on this, Lucas. They'd make great additions to the family, so take your time and do this right."

He gave his son a mock punch in the arm as he went to the mudroom to fetch a handful of small bags. "I'm going down to meet the ladies and scoop the poop. Be back in a few," he said as he headed to the deck. Lucas watched him leave with a bemused look on his face.

"Don't look so surprised, Luc. Dad and I could both see that Sherri knocked you flat out the day you met her. It's a family trait. When we meet the right woman, we just know. When I met Alexis, I knew she was the one woman in the world for me. It's just how it works for us.

I knew at the wedding that it wouldn't be long before you'd be going down the same path. I told Alexis that Sherri needed to put on her running shoes because you were gonna chase her down until you got her."

Lucas gave a loud shout of laughter. "Thanks a lot. So I'm so ugly that I'm gonna have to ambush her, is that it?"

"No, that's not what I'm saying at all," Jared replied. "I mean, yeah, you're ugly as homemade sin, but that's not why you've got your work cut out for you. Sherri had a really rough time when she got pregnant with Sydney. Sydney's father cut and ran as soon as he found out and he hasn't been back since. Her family wasn't any help at all. They pretty much turned their backs on her, so she was all alone trying to raise her child and finish school. If it hadn't been for Emily and Alexis and their mothers, I don't know how she would have done it," Jared said solemnly. "She hasn't had anything to do with the male species since then and if you're gonna be the first man she trusts enough to try again with, you better have your shit together. Alexis loves her like a sister and so do I, not to mention Miss Sydney. If anything happens to hurt the two of them, the consequences will be dire. And I'll be one of the first ones in line to extract retribution, so don't get it twisted, Lucas. This is not play time."

Lucas was running a damp mop over the hardwood floors in the kitchen and dining room while Jared was delivering his summation of the situation. He narrowed his eyes at his older brother and pulled his earlobe, a sure indication of his annoyance.

"What have I ever done to make you think that I'm some kind of pond scum–sucking lowlife who's going to subject Sherri and Sydney to emotional turmoil? Your track record was no better than mine before you met Alexis. I date a lot, sure, and I haven't gotten serious with anyone, but it's not because I'm a sociopath. And if memory serves, you hold the family record for the most women in a month, so you really don't have any grounds for lecturing me.

"I like Sherri a lot and I love Sydney and I do take this situation seriously, which is why I've been taking my time. I'm not trying to mess up their lives," he said heatedly. "I'm trying to make them both happy so I'd appreciate it if you step off. Give me some credit for having some common sense, you damned asshat," he muttered under his breath as he stowed the mop in the mudroom.

To add to his growing irritation, Jared was laughing when Lucas returned to the kitchen. "Now what? What's so freakin' funny?"

"I'm proud of you, Luc. You reacted the way I wanted you to, which let me know that you've got your head on straight. I think that you and Sherri are a good idea, a really good idea. But I'm not the one you have to convince. Your intentions are all in the right place, but Sherri's gonna take a lot of tender loving care if you want to make her your lady."

Just then the doors in the dining room opened and in raced the dogs, followed by Sydney and everyone else. Further conversation was impossible, so the only alternative was dessert. But while he was serving the strawberry shortcakes with homemade vanilla-bean ice cream, Lucas couldn't keep his eyes off Sherri. He'd fallen hard and fast for her. Lucas was a true VanBuren through and through because he knew at that moment he would do whatever it took to find the way to her heart.

Chapter 3

After the Mother's Day weekend, Sherri had a new perspective on a few things. For one thing, she was beginning to think that *date* wasn't a four-letter word after all, especially if the date was with Lucas VanBuren. He had many, many fine characteristics, but the most important of those attributes was the fact that he and Sydney already had a great friendship. Lucas genuinely cared for her little girl. She could see it every time he was around her. And they were around each other often, especially since the Hilton Head holiday.

He had joined their church and he always managed to sit with Sherri and Sydney. Because they routinely sat with Jared and Alexis, it was like being part of a big family, which was rather pleasant. After church they usually had dinner together as a group, especially when the elder VanBurens were in town. Lucas had finally convinced her to go out with him, and they'd had several dates, although their outings always included Sydney. They had gone to the movies, to an amusement park and on a couple of picnics with Alexis's little dogs, Sookie and Honeybee. Sydney had a ball every time, and Sherri found herself getting more and more comfortable with Lucas. And now they were going on their first couple-only date, a momentous and, for Sherri, completely unforeseen occasion.

Alexis was beyond pleased with the situation and she continued to express her joy the whole time she was doing Sherri's hair the day of the big event. They were in Alexis's private styling area at Sanctuary One, the flagship location of the posh spas Alexis had owned for several years. After giving her friend's thick hair a touch-up and a trim, she had blown her dry and was styling it with the aid of a ceramic flat iron.

"I can't believe you've finally come to your senses. It's about time you started acting like a real woman. Hooking up with a real man like Lucas is just what you need," she gloated.

"Alexis, give it a rest! You're repeating yourself, for one thing. That's the third time you've said that real woman–real man thing. And nobody said anything about hooking up in the slutty way. We're going to the recital and because Sydney's going to a sleepover after,

Lucas and I are going out. It's not the beginning of the world or the end of it, so just chill, can't you?"

"Don't play with me," Alexis said sternly. "I have some real hot curling irons within striking distance of your stubborn head, so now isn't the time for messing around."

Sherri felt her cheeks getting warm—not because of the aforementioned hot irons, but because Alexis had hit on the real truth of the matter. As much as she tried to deny it, there was more to this date than hanging out with a good friend. Every time she was around Lucas she experienced all kinds of sensations, and not just the warm, fuzzy, family-friend kind. This was the other part of the new perspective she'd gained from spending friendly time with Lucas. Her sex drive wasn't totally dormant after all. She'd been telling herself that she simply had no desire for a man, but the way she reacted to Lucas's touch was telling her the truth. There was something about Lucas that constantly reminded her that she was a woman—a fully functioning woman with the same desires as any other healthy female. The sensation was both exhilarating and intimidating, and although she was reluctant to talk about it to Alexis, she wasn't going to run away from it. But she did plan to downplay the big event to Alexis. She knew her friend would tease her relentlessly to the point of making her nervous, which she didn't want, not at all. All she wanted was a nice, relaxing evening with a friend. Surely that wasn't too much to ask for, right?

"So where are you going? What are you going to wear?" Alexis was eager for every detail as she finished styling Sherri's chic bob.

"I'm not sure. He said it was a surprise. We're going after Sydney's dance recital so whatever I wear to that is what I'll have on. And that's that," she said airily.

Alexis looked mildly frustrated. "This isn't fair. You stayed all up in my business when I was dating Jared and you won't even toss me a crumb about Lucas, my own brother-in-law. How selfish can you be?"

Sherri grinned unrepentantly. "Pretty darned selfish, I freely admit it. Yes, I did get all up in your Kool-Aid when you were dating Jared, and I got all in Emily's business with Todd, but that was different."

"How was that different? Lean back so I can take a weed whacker to those shrubs over your eyes," Alexis ordered.

"It was different because I was being the voice of reason for you two. Y'all were in love and you needed an objective viewpoint from a concerned and loving friend. It's not like that with me and Lucas. We're just two friends enjoying each other's company. *Ouch!*"

"Don't be a baby—you've had your eyebrows waxed before," Alexis scolded.

"It never hurt like that," Sherri protested. "You did that on purpose to get information out of me, but I keep telling you—there is none. We'll probably go get something to eat after the recital and that'll be the end of it."

Alexis opened her mouth to let her friend in on the

fact that Lucas was after something much more than a casual friendship, but she prudently changed her mind. When Sherri figured it out for herself they'd have plenty to talk about. Then she'd get to be the voice of reason for her intelligent but unaware friend. She smiled at her reflection in the mirror as she finished Sherri's brows.

The dance recital had been a smashing success, mostly because of the adorable little dancers in their clever costumes but partly because Lucas had contributed the refreshments. He'd arranged for a vast array of canapés and desserts to be delivered from Seven-Seventeen, the fine dining restaurant owned by the brothers VanBuren, and he had also provided staff to set up, serve and clean up afterward. He'd made quite an impression on the dance moms—and not just for his generosity. Several of the women in attendance had given him the once-over, devouring him with their eyes.

Sherri had overheard one of the older dancers ask Sydney if he was her mom's boyfriend and Sydney had answered "yes," which was both endearing and alarming to Sherri. She was going to have to have a little chat with her daughter soon, that much was obvious. But for now, she was just going to enjoy the evening.

It was off to a great start. When Lucas came to pick her up at her condo promptly at nine, he was not only looking and smelling good, but he'd also brought her a big green plant. He'd insisted on picking her up at her condo rather than having her follow him to the site of their outing.

"When I take a lady out, I pick her up and bring her home. I know it's old school, but that's how I roll. You don't mind, do you?"

When he looked down at her with his long-lashed eyes sparkling and his ridiculously sexy smile, she couldn't think of a single reason to protest the arrangement. She'd driven home from the dance studio in minutes and even changed clothes, taking off the coffee-colored slacks and matching blouse she'd worn. Now she was wearing a hot orange tank dress made of a supple rayon knit fabric that showed off her slender figure and her legs. Because he was much taller than she was, she could wear her bronze strappy sandals with the four-inch heels and not worry about towering over him; she still barely reached his shoulder.

Sherri never wore a lot of makeup, but she'd added a little blush and lipstick, along with another coat of mascara and a bit of smoky eye shadow. A pair of big gold hoop earrings and an armful of Indian bangle bracelets in gold with bright pops of color completed her ensemble. When she saw the smile on Lucas's face, she was glad she'd made the effort. He'd changed clothes, too, she noticed. He was now wearing a pair of dark slacks and a really nice shirt that brought out his green eyes nicely. It was her turn to smile as she held out her hands for the plant.

"Lucas, this is a beautiful ficus," she said. "It's so sweet of you."

He ignored her outstretched hands and took the big plant over to the window, placing it gently on the floor. "It's heavier than it looks," he said. "And you look gorgeous, by the way."

"Thank you. I was just thinking the same about you," she answered with a smile.

The smiles continued as the evening progressed. First they went to a restaurant called Sweet Tea and 3 Sides. It was a barbecue joint that had some of the best food in town. As soon as they walked in the door people were calling her name, waving at her and, in a few cases, coming up to give her a hug. After they were seated, Lucas began laughing softly.

"What's so funny?" Sherri asked.

"I was laughing at myself because I wasn't sure you'd like this place, but ever since we came in the door it's like being with a celebrity. Do you know everybody in Columbia?"

Sherri grinned as she shook her head. "I don't know everybody in Columbia, but I do treat a lot of children so a lot of people know me as Dr. Sherri. I have my regular practice and I work at the free clinic, too. And more to the point, I love barbecue. I love to eat it, but I don't like to grill, so I'm here at least twice a month," she told him.

Just then their server arrived with menus and big glasses of sweet tea. After greeting Lucas, the young woman asked if he wanted to look at the menu or if he'd be having what Dr. Sherri was having. Sherri laughed sheepishly. "Okay, so maybe I'm in here more than twice a month. Like almost every weekend," she admitted. "But the food is so good, I can't resist."

After placing their orders, Lucas reached across the table to take her hand. "You don't have to explain. I'm a fiend for good barbecue and, luckily, I like to grill so I'll make some for you whenever you want. And I agree that the food here is excellent. I've eaten here several times."

They chatted companionably over dinner and shared a big portion of blackberry cobbler for dessert. She looked so animated and pretty that Lucas asked what she was thinking about.

"I was thinking that this is the best date ever," she told him before licking the last of the cobbler off her spoon. "If I'd known how much fun this was I would have started dating a while ago."

"I'm glad you didn't," Lucas countered. "I'm glad I'm the one you allowed to have the pleasure of your company. And I hope you aren't tired because I have something else planned for us."

She didn't have to wait long to find out what he had in mind. After taking care of their check and leaving a generous tip for their server, Lucas started driving them to a club. He turned to Sherri as he drove and said, "I hope you like music." She assured him that she did.

"Good, because the place we're going to has some of the best blues I've ever heard."

The name of the club was Night Flight. The music was great; a singer who sounded just like the late Katie Webster was performing. Between sets a DJ played a mix of blues standards and jazz and when Lucas asked if she wanted to dance, Sherri gladly accepted. She used to love to dance, but she didn't get to do it very often except in her Zumba class or when she and Sydney were playing with the Wii. Dancing with Lucas was a totally different experience. Feeling his big arms wrapped around her as they moved to the music was really, really nice. She loved the way he smelled and the warmth of his body. She relaxed into his strong, muscular arms and everything dropped away from her consciousness, everything except the way her body felt pressed against his.

When the song ended she felt slightly disoriented for a moment. She didn't want to let go of the feeling of being surrounded by Lucas, but once the music stopped she had no choice in the matter. Back at their table she sipped her ginger ale and looked at Lucas, really looked at him, examining every bit of his face. He gave her a slow smile and leaned over so that she could hear him over the music and loud talking. With his lips touching her earlobe, he said, "You're looking at me awfully hard. Do I scare you or something?"

A sensation she hadn't felt since the night Sydney was conceived washed over her like the spray of a warm, gentle shower. She held perfectly still so he wouldn't see her trembling. "That would be 'or something,'" she murmured. This time her lips brushed against his ear because it was the only way he'd be able to hear her soft voice.

An odd expression raced across his face, replaced almost immediately by a big grin. "Let's get out of here so we can talk about it. Is that okay with you?"

She nodded and he rose to hold her chair. As they left Night Flight, her hand slid into his like they'd been holding hands for years. They drove to her condo in relative silence, although the idea was that they were supposed to be talking. In a short time they arrived in her gated complex, and he once again opened her door for her and took her hand as they walked to the house. If he'd been expecting her to give him a demure and chaste thank-you and good-night in the doorway, Lucas was mistaken. Sherri calmly opened the door and invited him in, saying she'd make iced coffee. And just like that, the two of them were alone in the house, together.

Chapter 4

Lucas couldn't believe his good fortune. This was what he'd wanted ever since he'd first seen Sherri back in February at his brother's wedding. He was alone with Sherri and could start the enjoyable process of getting to know her. It had taken weeks of anticipation, repeated invitations and a study guide provided by her brilliant daughter. Sydney was the one who'd told him that her mother loved barbecue, live music and green plants. He smiled at his reflection in the mirror as he washed his hands in the half bath off the living room.

"She gets sad when flowers die, Uncle Lucas. She likes big green plants. We have a lot of them in our condo, so if you want to bring her something, make it a plant. Like a ficus tree—she really likes those."

He owed Sydney big-time for the heads-up, he reflected. Sherri seemed to have enjoyed their evening, both the restaurant and the club, although Lucas was particularly happy with the latter. Holding her close to his body while they danced had been arousing in the extreme and he couldn't wait to do it again. The fact that she'd invited him to come in instead of bolting from him at the door was also a good sign. He dried his hands on the guest towel and went to join Sherri in the kitchen. The sound of the late Percy Mayfield's voice floated from her stereo speakers and created the perfect ambience for the night.

Once again he noted that she was a beautiful woman, totally striking even though she was just making tall glasses of iced coffee in her bare feet. Lucas loved a woman who could be herself in front of him; something as simple as taking off her fancy sandals to reveal her long sexy feet was a turn-on for him.

"Are you sure I can't help you with anything?" he asked as he seated himself at the long counter to watch her in action.

"I'm positive. The coffee is already in the refrigerator," she confessed. "I'm rather addicted to it and after I drink my morning cup I refrigerate it so I can have iced coffee in the evening. All I have to do is put a little cream and sugar and some coffee ice cubes and voilà, it's all done. You don't mind sugar in your coffee, do you?"

"It's fine," he assured her. "I like my coffee sweet. The ice cubes are a clever idea."

She didn't answer for a moment while she mixed cream and sugar, which she had put into a shaker jar, into the coffee. As she shook it up she told him it wasn't her own idea. "I saw them do it on the Food Network or I got it out of a magazine or something. But I love using them. They keep your drink cold without making it watery." She filled two tall glasses with the ice and poured the drinks. Placing them on a tray with a plate of mocha brownies, she turned to him and suggested they go to the living room.

Lucas got up to carry the tray and soon they were seated on her comfortable taupe sofa with the refreshments within easy reach on the coffee table. He took a sip of his drink and smiled his approval. "What else did you put in here? It's delicious."

"Some of your sister-in-law's homemade vanilla bean liqueur. Alexis is really clever about that kind of thing."

"Alexis is a gem," Lucas agreed. "But I don't want to talk about her."

"Okay. So what do you want to talk about?"

Lucas put his glass on the tray and held out his hand to Sherri. "I want to talk about you," he said. "The more I'm around you, the less I seem to know about you. I want to know you better. A lot better."

Sherri's eyes widened as she took in what he'd just said. "We do know each other, Lucas. I know that you have two brothers, Jared and your twin, Damon. I know that you have two sisters, Tamara and Camilla. Tamara is a doctor and Camilla is a commercial interior designer who specializes in restaurants. I know your parents and your grandmother. You're not exactly a mystery to me, Lucas."

As she was talking, she put her glass down next to his and placed her hand in the one he was holding out to her. He raised his eyebrows and said, "Yeah, you have a lot of information about me. I can only assume that you've been talking to my grandmother, because nothing is a secret with her."

Sherri laughed and admitted that most of her intel actually came from Alexis. "She's very chatty and she's told me quite a bit about the VanBuren family. But Ms. Delilah is no slouch either. When she found out that I don't have a man in my life she asked me if I preferred women," she said with a wicked grin.

"That's her to a tee." Lucas laughed. "What comes up comes out with her—she doesn't hold anything back. So, you know a lot about me, but I don't know nearly as much about you. I know you're a pediatrician, that you and Emily and Alexis are lifelong friends and that you have an amazing, engaging little girl. But aside from that I know nothing. Alexis might talk about my family in general, but she doesn't talk about you."

"God bless her," Sherri said wryly. "If she ever decided to run her mouth she could bury me because she knows everything there is to know about me." Her fingers were tracing patterns on Lucas's palm, very lightly, but with just enough pressure to start his temperature soaring. It felt good to have her touching him.

"I don't want to find out things secondhand. I want to know you better, but I want it on your terms. I don't want to pick up random bits of hearsay here and there. I want you to be able to tell me anything that's on your mind."

Sherri didn't answer him immediately. She continued her gentle exploration of his hand, inching up his forearm. "What is it that you want to know, Lucas?"

"Everything. Some of it's just mundane stuff, like what you like to eat, what you do for fun, what's your biggest vice. Some of it's really personal, like why you wanted to be a doctor, what your hopes are for the future and why Sydney's father seems to be missing in action."

To his surprise and utter gratification, Sherri moved a little closer to him. It wasn't a bold move—she didn't try to straddle him or anything. She just leaned in his direction in a graceful and subtle manner. He could feel her warmth and smell her delicate fragrance more strongly. Without making a big deal of it, he slid closer to her. She gave him a long, calculating look before she answered him.

"I'm not that interesting, really. I'm a total omnivore, for one thing. I will eat any and everything as long as it's prepared well. What I do for fun is pretty much what I do anyway. I take care of my baby and I try to always set a good example for her. I like to grow things, as you can see by all the plants around here. I also have a flower garden on the patio and we have a plot in the community garden where we grow vegetables," she told him. "As you can see, I'm pretty boring. I like music and plays and art and I love being a mommy. Now as far as my vices go, well, they're kind of embarrassing," she admitted.

Lucas was already intrigued and encouraged her to talk. "This is just between you and me, sweetheart. You can tell me anything."

"Okay, my vices are chocolate and potato chips. I've never met a potato chip I didn't love. Plain, salt and vinegar, lime-flavored, kettle chips, any kind you name, I love. I never bring them home because I don't want to hook my child on greasy junk food. But I'm an absolute sucker for potato chips. I also love chocolate, especially dark chocolate. In fact, if you've never had a wavy potato chip coated in chocolate you haven't lived," she said fervently.

Lucas burst out laughing. "I thought it was going to be something scandalous going by the look on your face. Potato chips? If you really like them, wait until you taste mine. I make the best chips in the world and I'll be happy to keep you supplied. And you're not the only one with weird food addictions. I'm a fiend for ice cream and I love pickles of any kind. In fact, I'm known for making pickles out of strange things like nectarines, radishes, plums, anything that looks good. So far you haven't revealed anything too strange," he said.

Sherri gave him an enigmatic smile and suddenly she

was even closer to him. Now she was using both of her hands in a constant massage that was sending electric shocks all over his body.

"I've always wanted to be a doctor," she offered. "When I was a little girl I hated to see anybody in pain or sick, and the doctors I saw when I was growing up always seemed to be grumpy and mean, so I decided that I'd be a doctor—a better doctor, one who could take care of people and make them feel better without making them cry. So that's my career story.

"I want Sydney to be independent, self-reliant, compassionate and successful, so my future plans revolve around being the best mother and role model I can be. Is that it for your inquiry?" She smiled when she said it, so he didn't think she had taken his interest in the wrong way.

"You're very open tonight and I really appreciate that," Lucas told her. "But I still don't know where Sydney's father fits into the picture."

Sherri's expression changed and her soothing fingers stopped moving. "That's because he's not in the picture. The last time I saw him was the day I told him that I was pregnant," she said in a cool voice. Pulling away from him, she sat back on the sofa and crossed her arms and her legs. "He dropped me like a hot rock and took off for parts unknown. I think he moved to California, but I wouldn't know because I never tried to find him."

"So he's never paid child support or done anything that would make it possible to see his child?"

"Not a thing in this world. I was scared when I found out I was going to have a baby. Terrified, really, because I'd worked so hard to finish medical school and it took up all my time and attention. I was doing well to have a boyfriend while I was trying to get through that first year as an intern and I didn't see how it was possible to have a baby and keep up with all the work. But from the moment I knew for sure I was carrying my baby, I knew I was going to have her.

"So I told my man that he was going to be a father and he went straight to Nutsville. He went on and on about how a man in his position couldn't afford the stigma of having an out-of-wedlock child and how his family would disown him and how he might get fired from the law firm where he had just started working. It wasn't a very productive conversation, as you can imagine."

Lucas gently uncrossed her arms and put his arm around her shoulders. "So what happened after that?"

"Absolutely nothing. I didn't hear from him for the next couple of days. I swallowed my pride and went to his apartment only to find that he'd moved out. The job he was so anxious to protect? He quit the job, left the apartment, left the city and the state. It was like he'd fallen off the earth."

"He is a fool," Lucas said with a savage edge to his voice. "You were without a doubt the best thing that ever happened to him and he just walked away from you and his child. Sydney is a very special kid. He has no idea what he's missing."

She made a ladylike snort of derision. "He's not the only one. My parents flipped out when they heard my news. Once they realized that I intended to keep my baby regardless of my lack of a husband, they pretty much turned their backs on me. They tolerate Sydney from time to time, but I haven't really let her spend much time with them ever since the day she came home and asked me what a little bastard was."

A dark red color surged up Lucas's neck and made his face blotchy. His anger was plain to see, and he couldn't keep his temper from coming out in his words. "Are you kidding me? They actually said that in front of her? What kind of people are they?"

Sherri's body relaxed and her head slid down to his shoulder. "My parents aren't bad people at all— they're just stuck-up and mired in their own importance. They're very upper-middle class and they strive to keep up appearances at all costs. They own a few funeral parlors and were concerned about the family image, especially when Daddy decided to run for city council. They really wanted me to marry Trevor. They thought that Trevor Barnes would be the perfect son-in-law, but then I ruined everything by acting like a little hood rat and getting pregnant."

She sighed deeply and rubbed against his broad shoulder before adding, "I still don't get the idea that I 'got' pregnant. I only brought the eggs. He brought the sperm and the cheap condoms so why doesn't he get half the blame? I didn't conceive my baby all on my own, and I was a medical student, for God's sake. It wasn't like I intended to get pregnant. I was on the Pill and I made him use a condom every single time so how she came to be, I have no clue. But," she said firmly, "I've never been happier about anything in my life. Sydney is truly my joy."

Lucas leaned over and kissed her. He'd been wanting to for months and he couldn't think of anything profound to add to what she'd said so he followed his instincts. His head bent to hers and he took his time, savoring the first touch of her soft, juicy mouth. That first soft pressure was followed by his tongue gently outlining the curve of her lips, teasing them open to receive him. She did so, parting her lips gently, opening wide enough to take his tongue against her own, allowing him to give her the pleasure she'd denied herself for so long. Their mouths mated like lovers who'd been away from each other for too long.

His hands cupped her face while hers stroked his shoulders, sliding up to his neck. Holding him gently but firmly, she allowed the kiss to deepen while their tongues did a long, sensual dance, stroking and tasting until it seemed as though they had done this many, many times. It could have gone on for minutes or hours— Lucas didn't know and he didn't care. All he knew at that moment was that he didn't want this kiss to end.

It had been months since they met, months in which

she'd occupied his thoughts and desires, and now she was in his arms. He was getting hot to the point where he thought for a moment they might burst into flames right there on her sofa. He began to slow his movements, gradually leading up to the moment that they would pull apart, but Sherri wasn't taking his cues. Incredibly, she seemed to be getting into it more and more, moving against him until her mounting desire was unmistakable.

He finally pulled away from her with great reluctance. The desire on her face was reflected in his own, and he could see her nipples pushing at the thin fabric of her dress. He wanted nothing more than to peel the dress and everything else off her body and make love to her all night long. But it was too soon. She deserved more than hasty, unplanned sex on their first date.

She turned so that she was kneeling next to him on the cushions of the sofa, and she put her arms around his neck. This time she initiated the kiss, using her sweet lips to coax him into submission. He let her have her way, sucking his lower lip gently before exploring his tongue with hers. In the parlance of the kitchen, she was sending him from a slow simmer to a rolling boil and before things got totally out of hand, he took control of the situation. He put his hands around her slender waist and stood up before carefully placing her on the floor.

"I know it's been a while for me, but you can't tell me that wasn't a good kiss," she said frankly.

With equal candor he replied, "It was one of the best,

if not the single best I've ever had. I stopped because I don't think you're ready for what comes next."

"I'm a doctor—nothing scares me."

Lucas laughed and flexed his fingers over her waist. They hadn't quite managed to let go of each other yet and he was running out of reasons to do so. This was a surprising turn in the evening's events. When he'd asked her out he hadn't had a minute-by-minute play-book in his head for how the evening should go, but he hadn't planned on her wickedly sensual response to him. There were many more pieces to the Sherri puzzle than he'd anticipated, but he was looking forward to finding them all.

"Sherri, sweetheart, I think I should go. I don't want to push you into something that you're not ready for and if I stay, I don't think we'll keep talking. I think we'll do everything but talk, as a matter of fact."

One silky brow went up in a quirky way as she considered his statement. "What makes you think I'm not ready? I admit it's been a while since I was sexually active, but the procedure is pretty standard, isn't it? I think we can handle it," she said in her damnably seductive voice as she moved closer to him, close enough that he knew she could feel the hard-as-steel erection with which he was now burdened.

"Listen, I freely admit that I'd like to make love to you more than I'd like to take my next breath, but it's not going to happen tonight. It's too soon, for one thing. This isn't something I want to rush into. I want to take my time and do it right. I wanted to kiss you. I've waited months for that kiss. But I can wait on everything else," he said softly, his deep voice rough with desire.

But Sherri wasn't through with him yet. "Suppose I don't want to wait?"

Lucas moved his hands to her shoulders and took a step back. Because his legs were long, it provided him with a lot of space between their bodies. "I don't have any condoms with me. If I can't protect you, I'm not going to bed with you. No buts," he added sternly as she opened her mouth to protest.

She gave him a mock pout as he all but dragged her to the door. "I hope you're not going to get all weird the next time I see you," she said.

"Definitely not," he assured her. "I hope you don't think about this after I leave and decide to never see me again."

"I'll see you tomorrow if you're working. I promised to take Sydney to Seven-Seventeen for dinner. Tomorrow morning is her swim class and then she endures getting her hair done so we go out to eat afterward. And I promise you, I won't be acting strange, not in the least."

The logical thing would have been to reach for the doorknob, but good healthy lust won out and Lucas pulled her into his arms for one last kiss. Their mouths fit together. He could feel his passion about to blaze like a flambé pan splashed with cognac. It was hard, fast and full of longing but extremely satisfying.

"I'm getting out of here while I still can. Good night, Sherri."

"Good night," she whispered.

Chapter 5

After locking the door behind Lucas, Sherri tidied up the living room. It should have taken just a few minutes, but she had too much on her mind. She had to draw on all of the analytical abilities she'd developed in years of college and med school for her to sort through what had just happened. As she took the tray into the kitchen, she tried to make sense of everything. She poured out the iced coffees and washed the glasses, then put the uneaten brownies into a ziplock bag. She opened the refrigerator to put them away after she removed one and took a big bite. Chocolate always helped her think more clearly.

On the one hand, it was no big deal, right? All she'd done was act like a normal, fully functioning woman for a change. She'd gone out with a handsome, very sexy guy and had a good time. He'd brought her home and they'd kissed a few times. No big whoop; this was just what her friends had been telling her to do for years and she'd finally done it. So what? She wiped off the counters in the kitchen, put away the wooden tray and glanced around to make sure that nothing was out of place. Taking a deep breath, she turned the lights off and went into the living room.

Everything was tidy, as usual, but that didn't stop her from fluffing every pillow on the sofa and two chairs, straightening every magazine and picking off every dead leaf on the many plants that adorned the room. She'd always been an organized person and now, with her active little girl and her busy career, it was paramount that she stayed on top of the mundane chores that kept the condo neat and homey. She paused by the ficus tree with its glossy leaves and smiled. It was such a nice addition to the greenery she and Sydney adored and it would always remind her of Lucas. And that was the other hand, the thing that made her current situation rather uncomfortable.

She plopped down on an ottoman near the stairs and looked at the pretty plant with a frown on her face. Of course it was normal for a healthy woman to enjoy a flirty night of dancing and kissing with a big hunk of man, but the whole thing had much more meaning for Sherri. Lucas was the first man she'd kissed since the night she and Trevor conceived Sydney. More to the point, he was the only man she'd wanted to kiss. Many men had pursued her over the years and she was always able to send them on their merry way without a second thought. Her priorities were firmly in place, as were her totally justifiable fears of abandonment.

She knew for a fact that men could be craven cowards who ran out on a woman rather than owning up to their responsibilities. After Trevor's betrayal and subsequent disappearance, she'd made herself a promise that she'd never, ever allow herself to get so caught up in a man that she put all her trust in him. They just weren't worth her trust—that's what she'd decided. And after Sydney's birth she'd renewed that vow with a codicil. She would never let any man get close enough to her or her precious baby. No man would ever have the chance to break her daughter's heart the way hers had been shattered by Trevor. Giving up a love life had been a very small sacrifice to make for Sydney's sake. Not once had she regretted choosing her little girl's happiness over sex. Not until the first time Lucas touched her hand.

She groaned loud and long, dropping her head into her hands. After a moment she had to laugh at herself. Pushing the ottoman back into its normal spot, she went to do her usual house check, turning off the music and then making sure that all the doors and windows were locked and that the alarm was set. Filling a thermal glass with ice and water, she went upstairs to bed. She undressed slowly and thoughtfully before getting into the shower. There was nothing like a hot shower to send her to sleep. Tonight, though, the shower did nothing but remind her of what Lucas's touch did to her. When the spray of hot water hit her skin it was like being stroked with his strong fingers over and over. All over. She directed the handheld shower over her body, lingering in all the places she wanted him to touch and to taste. With her eyes closed and the sweet scent of her body gel wafting up to her sensitive nose, all she could think about was what they'd be doing right now if not for the condom shortage.

She ended the shower with a punishing cold blast of water as though it could put an end to her wayward thoughts, but her ploy didn't succeed. Wrapped in a big pink towel, she sat on the edge of her bed and started applying the coconut oil she liked to use. The oil melted into her skin and gave it a delicious scent, which only increased her sexual angst. Who knew that all of her desires would come galloping back after one kiss? That wasn't strictly true, though; the second their hands connected something had happened to her deep inside. It only got more intense every time their skin made contact, and tonight was the most explosive reaction she'd ever registered. Even Trevor, who considered himself to be an accomplished lover, hadn't had the same effect on her libido.

Once she was moist from head to toe and smelling fantastic, she slid under the covers without a stitch on. Sleeping nude was one of her favorite things, although she didn't do it when Sydney was home. Normally she fell asleep as soon as her head hit the pillow, but tonight all she could think about was Lucas and what it would be like to have him next to her in the bed. A litany of "if onlys" went around and around in her head and she couldn't seem to cut them off. If only she wasn't convinced that sex couldn't be a part of her life. If only Lucas wasn't so damned sexy. If only he was a dimwit and a bore instead of such a charming man; she wouldn't be tossing and turning right now if he was a loser. She sat up straight and drank deeply from the glass of water before taking one of the cubes out and rubbing it down her throat and between her breasts. Like it or not, Lucas VanBuren's kiss had awakened something deep inside her psyche, something she hadn't realized was even there. She put her head back on the pillow, sure that she wasn't going to sleep that night.

Luckily she did manage to fall asleep, but her dreams were not only erotic, they were highly specific and centered on Lucas. She didn't have time to dwell on the X-rated cinema of her mind, though; today was a busy day. Sydney was ready and waiting to be picked up after her sleepover and she was her usual cheery, chatty self. After thanking her friend Lisa's mom for having her over, saying goodbye to Lisa and kissing her mother hello, Sydney was buckled into her seat in the car.

"Mommy, did you bring my swimsuit and things for swim class?"

"Of course I did, sweetie. Your bag is in the trunk and everything is in it."

Satisfied with her answer, Sydney plunged ahead to more important matters. "Did you have fun last night?"

Startled, Sherri's cheeks flamed as she was trying to formulate an answer, but Sydney kept talking.

"I mean did you have fun on your date with Uncle Lucas, Mommy. Where did you go? What did you do?"

"Oh, I wouldn't call it a date, Sydney. Lucas and I went to Sweet Tea and had barbecue and then we went to a club to listen to music and dance. Then he brought me home."

"That sounds like a date to me, Mommy. Did he come and pick you up?"

"Yes, he did."

"Did he bring you a present?"

"Well, he brought me a really pretty plant, but that's not exactly a gift, I don't think."

"He took you out to eat and he took you out to dance and he paid for everything, right?"

Sherri's eyes were brimming with laughter as she answered. Sydney might make a very good attorney one day if she kept up her interrogation skills. "Yes, he did. But that doesn't mean it's a date-date. It just means it was a friend-date."

"No, Mommy, you're wrong. That's a real date, trust me."

"What do you know about real dates, little one? Where are you getting your information?"

"Everybody knows that stuff, Mommy."

They had reached the athletic center where Alexis taught weekly swim classes, so further conversation was forestalled as they went in and joined the class. Sydney had so much fun that it wasn't until later, when she was getting her hair done at Sanctuary Two, that she brought up the subject again. This time she addressed Alexis in an innocent voice.

"Auntie Alexis, what's a date?" she asked sweetly.

Alexis was separating Sydney's abundant hair into four equal parts so that she could blow-dry each section. "A date is when two people who like each other spend time together."

"Did you and Uncle Jared go on dates before you got married?"

"Sure we did, cutie. We went on lots of dates."

"Did he pick you up and bring you a present and take you somewhere and pay for everything?"

Alexis smiled at her warmly and agreed that, yes, he had. Sydney gave her mother a triumphant grin and said, "See? I told you, Mommy. That was a real date you had with Uncle Lucas. I told you so."

Sherri was glad that they were in the private area Alexis used for her clients. If they'd been in the main styling area the whole salon would have heard her business being announced.

Alexis could tell by the look on Sherri's face that there was more to the story. Giving her friend the look that meant that a long session of girl talk was on the agenda for later that day, Alexis grinned and said, "You're absolutely right, cupcake. It was a real date and I'll bet they both had a great time. And Mommy's going to tell me everything as soon as I get done with your hair."

Sherri suddenly got really interested in her magazine and pretended that she didn't hear the two of them chattering away. But behind the cover of the latest issue of *InStyle,* she hid a secret smile.

Chapter 6

A week later, Lucas drove over to Sherri's condo to pick her up for what would be their second official date. He was in a great mood for several reasons, not the least of which was that he'd gotten his beloved Land Rover Defender back from Alana's Custom Classics. It was a vintage ride, a 1985 model, and before Alana put her loving and skilled hands on it, it was a hot mess of dents, scratches, patches of rust, Bondo and primer. Despite its appearance, he loved the boxy SUV with the ladders on the rear and the equipment rack that surrounded the entire roof. It had always been his intention to have the vehicle restored, but when he acquired it he lacked the money and now that he had plenty of money, he had no time. But Alana had taken one look at it and eagerly offered her services to bring it back to life. When he saw the spectacular results of her work, he was stunned.

"Alana, this is amazing. I knew Jared had done the right thing marrying your sister. You Sharp women are not only beautiful and smart, you're also talented. The man you marry is gonna be one lucky guy."

Alana merely smiled and replied, "The man I'm going to marry is a figment of your imagination. Go enjoy your ride."

He had the perfect idea for inaugurating the remodeled vehicle, and he was happy that Sherri agreed with him. He'd managed to get tickets to a jazz concert at the Spoleto Festival and she'd agreed to go with him. It was an annual event in Charleston that welcomed some of the most acclaimed artists in the world in dance, music, art and theater and he was looking forward to going. He was surprised that Sydney had declined his invitation, but she had other plans.

"Auntie Alexis is going to make jam and jelly this weekend, and I'm going to help her. She can make all kinds of things and they're really good. She's going to teach me how," she said happily.

When he arrived at Sherri's condo, both ladies were ready to go. Sydney's overnight bag was packed, and she was eager to get started on her own adventure. Sherri was dressed casually in a pair of copper-colored linen shorts with a scalloped hem and a crisp matching blouse with cap sleeves. The fabric was lightly suffused with gold and she wore a narrow gold leather belt that showed off her slender waist. With her flat sandals and a minimum of makeup, she looked fresh, sexy and stylish—as usual. Thanks to Sydney's urging, they were on their way in minutes. She was eager to reach Alexis and Jared's house.

When they reached their destination, Sydney was the first one out of the car, running to the door to greet the couple and their bouncy little dogs. She was excited and hardly paid any attention to her mother and Lucas as they departed. But she did manage to give them each a big hug and a kiss. "Have a nice time! See you tomorrow," she said cheerily as she waved goodbye from the doorway.

"I'm glad you're here, sweetie, but are you sure you didn't want to go with your mom?" Alexis asked.

Sydney nodded her head vigorously. "Yes, I'm sure. I want to help you make jelly and play with Sookie and Honeybee. Besides, Uncle Lucas and Mommy need some alone time," she said, sounding much older than six-going-on-seven.

Alexis exchanged a look of surprise with Jared over Sydney's head. "*Alone* time? Where did you get that from, Sydney?"

"I got it out of my head, Auntie Alexis. They have to spend time together so they can get to know each other really good before they get married."

Alexis was walking toward the kitchen when Sydney imparted this information, and she froze in place like a statue before turning around to stare at the child. "Who's getting married?"

"Mommy and Uncle Lucas," Sydney answered. "Where's my apron?"

Alexis and Jared gave each other identical looks of total shock as Sydney got on a stool to wash her hands over the kitchen sink.

"Who says they're getting married, sweetie?" Jared asked in a gentle voice.

"*I* said it. I asked Uncle Lucas if he liked my mommy a whole, whole lot and he said yes and I said he should marry her because he'd be a really good husband for her, just like you are for Auntie Alexis. And now he's working on it so we can get married and be a family," she said confidently. "What kind of jelly are we making first?"

Alexis finally recovered her ability to speak and asked if Sherri knew about this plan.

"I didn't tell her yet because it's a surprise. But she'll know pretty soon."

Jared could see that his loving wife was about to pass out so he put his arms around her and held her tight. "I knew that being married to you was going to be wonderful, but I had no idea it would be this much fun."

"Fun? This could be a disaster and you know it," Alexis said in a low voice.

Jared kissed her soundly and assured her that everything would work out. "I told you that Lucas had that look in his eyes the first time he saw her, the look that said he meant business. Don't worry—they'll be just fine."

Lucas couldn't have been any more pleased with the new turn of events in his life. After their first date he'd endured a cold shower when he got home from Sherri's condo, but it wasn't the magical cure-all of legend for sexual needs. A cold shower was supposed to make all desire leave at once, and in truth, it normally did. There was nothing like getting doused in icy water to turn off the urge for sexual fulfillment, but the memory of Sherri in his arms was too strong. His body was still horny and restless, and dreams of sublime lovemaking with Sherri had taken up most of the night.

When he awoke the next morning he was filled with optimism. As far as he could see, their date had been as close to perfect as possible and he was looking forward to a repeat performance. Sherri wasn't indifferent to him by any means, and that was an excellent sign of more good things to come.

They had promised each other that there would be no awkwardness the next time they saw each other, and there hadn't been. Sherri and Sydney had come to Seven-Seventeen for a late lunch just like she said they would, and everything was perfectly normal. Better than normal, actually, because there was no denying that something very special had transpired the night before. Sherri had looked beautiful as always, wearing a peach-colored outfit of a short cotton skirt and a short-sleeved T-shirt. Sydney was always adorable, and even more so with her long braids swinging with every movement of her active body. She had greeted him with a kiss on the cheek and a big hug and urged him to give one to her mommy, too.

"She had a lot of fun on your date, Uncle Lucas. You should probably give her a little kiss," she said in the voice that she thought was a whisper.

To his surprise, Sherri had tilted her head to allow him to plant one on her cheek. She returned it with a smile. "Thanks again for the lovely evening," she said sweetly.

Just like that they had moved out of the friend zone into a place where romantic possibilities bloomed. He had wasted no time in advancing his agenda, and in the days that followed he spent quite a bit of time with the Stratton ladies. He'd cooked for them one evening in the loft apartment he took over from Jared after he married Alexis. The meal was a great hit with Sydney because he had made pizza. She was absorbed in every step of the process, and when he taught her how to toss the dough in the air like a real pizza maker, she had been in heaven.

There had been other outings, always with Sydney along as a chaperone because he knew better than to trust himself alone with Sherri just yet. He didn't want to take things to the next level until she knew that she could trust him completely, so the only recourse he had was to make sure that they were always around other people. The only difference was the addition of long passionate kisses when they said good-night. Lucas had briefly considered the notion that those first kisses were a fluke, but he was absolutely wrong. Every time their mouths met it was more delectable than the time before. A hot surge of desire would well up until there was nothing in the world but Sherri, the taste of her, the feel of her and his total lust for her. He'd learned how to break off the kiss, say a gruff good-night and get in his car before he did something in her doorway they'd both regret.

It had been both rewarding and frustrating, but his patience had paid off. Sherri was beginning to trust him, at least enough to go to Charleston with him. Normally he would have dreaded a two-hour drive with a woman, but he was enjoying this one immensely. He looked over at her, neat and pretty in the passenger seat, and she looked like she was enjoying herself, too. Without giving it a thought, he reached over and took her hand.

"I'm glad you decided to come with me," he said with a smile.

Sherri used her free hand to remove her sunglasses and returned his smile. "I'm glad you asked me. I haven't been to Spoleto in years. This is a real treat for me." She continued to look at him with an unguarded expression. "You have an absolutely lethal smile," she teased him.

"Lethal? Is that a compliment or a criticism?" He laughed as she gave his hand a gentle squeeze.

"It's a compliment, of course. You just have a really sexy smile. I hope I'm not stepping on some other lady's toes by being with you."

"Are you serious? I'm not in a relationship with anyone right now. Haven't been for a long time," he said firmly.

Sherri's mischievous side was out in full force, apparently, because she didn't give up. "Are you sure? You're way too tasty to be flying solo. Why aren't you involved with some nice lady? I imagine there're a lot of women who'd like an answer to that question. You have all the components anyone could want in a mate. You're good-looking, talented and ambitious and my little girl loves you, so that means you're pretty much perfect. What's the story, Lucas? C'mon, you can tell me," she coaxed. "How in the world is a man like you walking around unattached?"

Lucas laughed loudly at Sherri's bold statement. This had to be the most he'd heard from her at one time and the fact that the words and phrasing were warm with humor *and* flirtatious gave him a burst of enthusiastic encouragement. He seized the opportunity to gain more knowledge about the mystery that was Sherri.

"I should be asking you the same questions, sweetheart. How in the world is a stupendous woman like you going through life without a partner? As exceptional as you are, you should have a devoted husband who lives just to make you happy," he countered.

She made a funny face, then laughed at him. "We're not talking about me. This conversation is about you. We already know why I don't date. I had my heart broken and my dreams of romance smashed to itty-bitty pieces by a man who didn't want to own up to his responsibilities. Case closed. There's no need to put your hand in the fire when you know it's gonna burn you. And besides, I have a partner, or are you forgetting Miss Sydney?" She was smiling.

Lucas was relieved that he hadn't insulted her with his clumsy phrasing. She poked his big biceps with her forefinger as she continued to prod him. "So don't try to deflect this onto me. Tell me about Lucas. I'll bet you and Damon have had girls falling all over you since you were in grade school. Did you ever pretend to be each other to trick people?"

"Yes, I confess we did. It's one of the perks of being identical twins, but we never did it to get over on a female, not deliberately. But we were pretty mischievous—I'm not gonna lie. Jared called us Demon and Lucifer for a reason, trust me."

Between their shared stories and laughter, the trip to Charleston seemed to take much less time, especially because Lucas never took his hand from hers the whole ride. They continued to hold hands as they walked around Charleston, enjoying everything about the festival. There was a lot to see. They toured art galleries, bought souvenirs for Sydney and saw as many sights as possible before having a delicious lunch of shrimp BLTs and she-crab soup at a popular restaurant.

The concert was outstanding, better than anticipated. The drive back to Columbia could have been a pain because of all the traffic, but nothing dimmed their good moods. They were engaged in conversation. The trip seemed to take no time at all.

When they arrived at Sherri's condo, Lucas carried in the bags and Sherri took them to Sydney's room. She returned to the living room to find Lucas in the kitchen pouring them each a glass of wine.

"Sorry if I'm being presumptuous," he said as he handed her a glass.

"Don't be silly," Sherri said as she took a glass from his hand. "This is a good idea. Are you hungry?"

He waited until she took a sip before leaning down to kiss her, slowly and with great intent. "No, I'm not hungry for food, sweetheart. I'm really hungry for something else, though, so I'd better get going."

His hands were warm on her shoulders, his fingers gently flexing as his thumbs moved in slow circles. She carefully put her wineglass on the counter and moved in closer to his warm body. Wrapping her arms around his waist she stood on her tiptoes to return the kiss with interest. She gave him more than he was expecting, using her tongue to tease the corners of his mouth before drawing his lower lip into her mouth and sucking on it gently. Before getting completely lost in the kiss she whispered, "I don't want you to leave."

Chapter 7

His hands slid down to cup her butt, and he lifted her easily as her legs went around his waist. Their mouths opened as one and their tongues started the sensual thrust and stroke that began the dance. The heat rose as Lucas walked with her into the living room. He went to the sofa and lowered their bodies so that he was lying on a pile of throw pillows with her slim body on top of his. Their mouths were still connected as his hands became acquainted with her body. He was touching her everywhere as the kiss gradually ended. Sherri's hands were equally busy until she lifted her head and looked at him quizzically.

"How did we end up here?"

"I didn't know how to get to your bedroom," he admitted.

"I can show you," she murmured. "Let's go."

Moments later they had gone up the stairs and entered her pretty bedroom with the taupe walls and champagne-colored duvet and curtains. The only light in the room was the moonlight filtering in through the sheers. It was more than enough for him to see their surroundings. There were peach and coral pillows on the king-size bed and window seat that matched a small velvet armchair and matching ottoman in the corner. The room was feminine and sexy, but it could have been a hunting cabin with a cot and Lucas wouldn't have cared. He was where he'd wanted to be for a long time and his total focus was on Sherri. Interior decoration was nowhere on his radar at the moment. All he cared about was the sexy woman who was taking off her sandals while he watched.

Her belt came next. He was fascinated by the slow precise way she undid the buckle before gracefully removing it. He pulled his own shirt free of his jeans and unbuttoned it while she did the same to hers.

She stopped before removing her linen shirt and gave him a self-deprecating grin. "I have to warn you about something," she said softly.

He met her eyes.

"I don't own any fancy underwear," she confessed. "It's all basic white cotton." She opened her blouse to reveal a plain white bra. A few seconds later, the matching bikini panties came into view as she divested herself of her shorts. It looked as cute as hell to Lucas; he'd had a lot of experience with the Victoria's Secret crowd and none of them had looked as sexy as she did right now.

His shirt fell to the floor and his jeans and boxers joined it as he held out his hand to Sherri. "You look perfect to me. Come here and let me show you just how gorgeous you are."

She put her long, slim hand into his and sighed as he pulled her into his arms. They held each other tightly until she gasped with surprise when she realized that he'd unhooked her bra and it was dangling from his fingertips.

"Wow. You're good."

"You have no idea," he growled, lifting her up once again. He managed to pull back the duvet and placed her on the huge firm bed. Before he joined her he reached in the pocket of his jeans and pulled out the condoms he'd taken to carrying at all times.

They reached for each other at the same time, each one touching the other the way they'd wanted, exploring the feel of each other's bodies. He bent his head to her breasts, taking one in his mouth, tasting her hardened nipple for the first time. Her fingers slid into his thick, wavy hair and she held him in place, sighing with pleasure while Lucas demonstrated his dexterity again by removing her panties in one smooth motion. His fingers eagerly explored her femininity, finding her wet. She moaned softly, and he turned his attention to her other breast, lavishing the tender tip with his tongue, then applying a firm suction that made her sounds of pleasure louder.

When he felt the moisture between her legs start to flow, the movements of his fingers became more deliberate. He stroked her over and over until her hips began to move and he felt her inner walls tighten. His mouth started traveling down her body, licking and tasting every inch of her. When he knew she was starting to climax, his mouth replaced his fingers and he held her hips while he treated her to the most intimate kiss possible, using his tongue and his lips to coax her to a series of orgasms that made her cry out in release. He couldn't stop tasting her, drinking her, devouring everything that made her a woman. She tasted like strawberries. All he knew at that moment was that he wanted to do this to her as often as possible. Giving her pleasure was the only thing he wanted.

He finally relented and began to kiss his way back up to her mouth while she trembled all over from the sweet torture. He rolled over onto his back and brought her on top of him, holding her close. As the rapid beating of her heart gradually slowed, she rubbed her face against his chest while her hand moved up and down against his hot skin. It was her turn to learn his body, to learn what brought him pleasure. She brought her hand down to his manhood, exploring his huge erection. Her hand slid up and down, cupping him gently yet firmly.

He reached for a condom and she took it from him, rolling it on. Now it was time for them to become one.

Lucas held her hips and guided her on top. She gripped his shoulders as he entered her body, gasping aloud as he gradually filled her to the brim. It took them a moment to find the right rhythm and after that their passion took over and the real mating began. One push turned into another and another, and they rocked back and forth in a heated frenzy. Lucas was taken over by Sherri in a way he'd never experienced with another woman. She was hot and sweet. He felt the explosion coming before he was ready to finish. He held her smooth hips as she moved against him, and he groaned her name aloud. When she tightened on his manhood, their voices mingled in a shattering climax that sent waves of satisfaction over both of them. This time they collapsed, wet with fulfillment and totally happy. It was a long time before either one of them could speak.

"Did I hurt you?" He stroked her hair as she slowly rubbed her face against his chest.

"Absolutely not." Sherri sighed. "That was amazing, Lucas."

"You're amazing, sweetheart."

She gave a soft, sleepy laugh. "I love the way you say that word. When you call me that I think I really am your sweetheart."

"You are," he answered, but she didn't hear him; she had drifted into sleep.

* * *

After the loving was a classic opportunity for embarrassment, regrets and the time-dishonored walk of shame, but none of those things happened. After sleeping in each other's arms, Sherri was awakened by Lucas with a repeat performance that left her more than satisfied. They showered together, shared grilled cheese sandwiches and finished the rest of their wine. They saw no reason to not go back to bed. This time was more romantic—Sherri had lit some candles and Lucas put on some sexy jazz. They talked and made love until sleep claimed them again.

He had to leave early the following day because he was working the early shift at Seven-Seventeen. Before he left, he fixed breakfast for Sherri and brought it to her in bed. He kissed her goodbye and told her he would call her later. She felt well-rested and relaxed. The profound sense of well-being made her smile.

It had been a long time since she'd been with a man. Trevor's obnoxious behavior after finding out that she was pregnant had soured her on men, even though she'd denied the idea when her friends brought it up. She'd always told them that she was waiting for Sydney to get older before she tried the dating scene again, but it was a half-truth. She had truly loved Trevor, or at least that was what she'd thought at the time. Finding herself pregnant and alone as she began her internship had been devastating and difficult.

There had been times when she didn't think she was

going to be able to accomplish her goals and still have a healthy, happy baby, but she had. The fact that her parents had turned their backs on her when she refused to abort her child or give it up for adoption could have crushed her spirit permanently, but with the loving support and assistance of her friends and their mothers, she'd made it through the toughest part of her life so far. Doing without male companionship wasn't a sacrifice at all. She felt fulfilled with Sydney. Her life was balanced between caring for her child and her medical practice, and she was satisfied. No matter what Alexis and Emily said about the need for her to have a social life and a sex life, Sherri was happy with the way things were. At least she had been until Lucas had entered her life.

Just the thought of him made her glow inside and out. He was good to look at; that was undeniable. The way his green eyes lit up when he smiled always made a little thrill race down her spine. He was also sexy as hell. She'd known that from the first time he held her hand, and last night had only served to underscore everything she'd sensed about his prowess. Trevor had been her first and only lover, and compared to Lucas he'd been like a teenager fumbling around in the backseat of his father's car. There was absolutely no way to compare the experience she'd shared with Lucas to what she'd had with the man who'd fathered her child—no way in this world.

Lucas was kind and thoughtful and he treated her daughter like a little princess. He was the type of man who'd make a wonderful family man if he ever decided to settle down. There wasn't anything about him that she didn't like, from his easy conversation to the genuine warmth of his personality. They might have just moved into the friends-with-benefits stage, but his presence in her life was a wonderful, albeit surprising change in her life and she was going to enjoy it for as long as it lasted.

After her breakfast she decided to take a long bubble bath before going to get Sydney from Alexis's house. Once the bedroom had been returned to its normal pristine condition, she got dressed and took a good look in the mirror at the finished result. Even to her own critical eye, she looked good. There was something to be said for sharing a night of lovemaking with a handsome man. Emily and Alexis had been right about one thing for sure—she'd been denying herself for too long and that was a mistake she wasn't going to make again.

She opened the front door, and to her surprise there stood Alexis, her finger poised to push the doorbell. Sydney was standing next to her, holding Sookie's and Honeybee's leashes. All three of them were giving her big happy smiles and they looked totally adorable, like a greeting card.

"Hello, ladies. I was just coming to get Sydney. Did you have fun yesterday? Were you a good girl?"

"Yes, I was, Mommy. We had a lot of fun. We're going outside," she added as she and the dogs came in the front door and took off for the dining room to get out on the deck.

Alexis also entered the condo, but she paused to give Sherri a pretty gift bag and a smug smile. "I think it's time for a little girl talk, don't you?"

Sherri had to laugh as she bowed to the inevitable. "Come on in the kitchen and I'll make you some coffee. I was wondering when you'd ferret your way all up in my business."

"And you know this," Alexis said. "It's a BFF prerogative."

Chapter 8

Lucas had to endure a Q&A from Jared the morning after his night with Sherri. He was in the back office at Seven-Seventeen going over invoices when his older brother came in and gave him a once-over before sitting down across from him.

"I don't have to ask if you had a good time with Sherri. I can see it all over your face."

"Yes, I did. She's everything, Jared. She's the one."

"That's good to hear because Sydney is planning the wedding and I'd hate for her to be disappointed."

Lucas let out a shout of laughter. "She won't be. She's something else, isn't she?"

"She told us about her plan to get her mommy married off to you. That little girl has all the planning and precision of a corporate raider or something," he said, shaking his head. "If I ever have a small country to invade or a government to overthrow, she's the first one I'm going to consult. But she's totally serious, Lucas. Are you ready for this?"

Lucas leaned back in his big swivel chair and laced his fingers together behind his head. "Ready, willing and able, big brother. I'm not playing around with Sherri—I want to marry her. I haven't asked her yet because I don't want her to think I'm crazy, but as far as I'm concerned it's a done deal. Meeting Sherri was like finding the other half of my soul, man. I don't have to tell you—the same thing happened to you when you met Alexis so you know where I'm coming from."

"It's a family characteristic." Jared laughed. "It happened to Dad, it happened to me and now it's your turn. And the next time it'll be Damon, once he opens his mind to something other than being the perfect dad. So how does Sherri feel about all this?"

Lucas sat up and put his arms on the desk. His face took on the unmistakable look of a man who was completely in charge of his destiny. "She's going to love it, every bit of it. I'm trying to take my time so she won't feel overwhelmed, but by the end of summer, it'll be a done deal."

"Go for it, man. It'll be nice to have her in the family. And Sydney might have a little cousin on the way by then, too," he added with a grin.

Lucas raised his eyebrows and lifted his hand to give

Jared a high five. He repeated his brother's words with a grin. "Go for it."

"Just think, next year this time it could be you getting ready for fatherhood. Can you handle that?" he asked in a teasing tone of voice.

"Bring it on," Lucas replied with a cocky grin. "I'm ready for anything and everything as long as I've got Sherri and Sydney."

Alexis refused the coffee Sherri offered and asked for lemonade instead. Her eyes were lit up with mischief as Sherri opened the gift bag and took out three exquisite bras with matching panties. Her face turned a deep pink as Alexis burst into laughter.

"These were supposed to be for your birthday, but I have a feeling that you need them now. Once you cross over into the sexy side you need to have something other than those schoolgirl undies you love so much."

Sherri was examining the pretty garments with awe, exclaiming over the sexy cut of the thongs and fingering the soft bras in mocha, peach and black. She stopped long enough to refute Alexis's last statement.

"They're not schoolgirl—they're practical. An intern who's also a new mother can't afford a drawer full of Vicky's Secret. They're inexpensive and easy to machine wash, which is all I require in underwear," Sherri argued.

"Not anymore. You did a lot more than go to a jazz concert, didn't you? So now you're going to need a drawer full of pretty things so you can show off for your man," Alexis gloated.

Sherri tried to play coy but she knew it was fruitless. She thanked Alexis for the gift and tried to distract her by offering her toast. "Did you bring me some jam? You know I can't eat the store-bought kind anymore."

"Yes, we brought you some. We made grape jam and apple butter, and Sydney was totally in heaven. She's an excellent little helper, as you already know. And yes, I'd like some toast but that doesn't get you off the hook. I need details, woman. You can't lie to me—I've known you too long for that."

Sherri got out the bread and butter while Alexis was demanding information. As she placed two slices of the special English muffin bread she favored in the toaster, she finally answered her friend.

"Everything was wonderful, Lexie. The drive to Charleston, the festival, lunch, the concert—everything was just perfect. And yes, we spent the night together and it was, it was..." She paused while she tried to think of the right words to use. "It was sublime," she said finally. The toast popped up at the same time as if to underscore her statement, and she had to stifle a giggle. She buttered the toast and put the slices on a plate. Alexis was too busy clapping her hands to take it from her so Sherri opened the jar of apple butter and spread some on a piece. She was about to take a bite when Alexis snagged it from her fingers.

"I knew it," Alexis said, gesturing with her prize.

"As soon as you opened the door, I knew. You look like a different person, Sherri. You and Lucas make such a great couple," she gushed. "This is what Emily and I have wanted for you, girl. Tell me everything and don't leave out a single detail. Well, some really private details you can keep to yourself, but I want the highlights at least."

"Slow your roll, chick. Nobody said anything about being a couple, not really. Friends with benefits—isn't that what they call it these days?"

Alexis rolled her eyes and helped herself to the second piece of toast. "Can I have some more lemonade? And do you have any cantaloupe? I can't seem to stop eating it. And don't be ridiculous—of course you're a couple. Tell me everything that happened and I'll prove it to you," she added as she slid off the tall stool by the work island and went to the refrigerator to find fruit.

Sherri's expression turned dreamy-eyed as she described the trip to Charleston and the parts of the night she felt comfortable sharing. "It was…amazing, Lexie. I can't even explain how amazing it was." She sighed.

Alexis came back to the work island with a bowl of cantaloupe chunks she'd scavenged from the fridge. She gave Sherri a quick but heartfelt hug. "You don't have to explain. I've got a VanBuren of my own, remember?"

"Yes, but you two are a couple, a for-real married couple. It's hardly the same thing. Lucas is sweet and sexy and just wonderful, but he hasn't said anything about wanting to be my man or anything like that." She was about to keep going but the doorbell rang.

She came back to the kitchen with a big orchid in a beautiful peach color and a slightly dazed expression. Alexis's eyes brightened with merriment.

"That's really pretty. Is it from anyone we know?"

"It's from Lucas. And there's a giant ficus in the living room, which was way too big for me to move. It's beautiful," she said with a little sigh.

Alexis took note of Sherri's bemused state and said gently, "I know it's been way too long for you to remember clearly, but this is how couples behave. As a matter of fact, I remember getting a beauty of a plant from Jared the morning after. He brought me red roses on our first date, and he sent me a huge plant the next morning. And I remember that you were very impressed and you teased me about finding my soul mate. It looks like you've found yours, too."

Sherri's eyes moved from her exotic floral tribute to her friend. "Alexis, I think you're jumping the gun here. Jared and Lucas are brothers, sure, but that doesn't mean that they act just alike. Just because Jared fell in love with you at first sight doesn't mean anything as far as Lucas is concerned. He's just being nice, and that's all."

"Sherri, I love you like a sister but you're acting dense. Someone who dishes out good advice on matters of the heart should be able to take it."

"What are you talking about?" Sherri's confusion was plain in her facial expression and her voice.

Alexis took pity on her friend, but only a little. "Sherri, my sistah, you do remember giving me and Emily a lot of advice when we were flailing around in the confusing throes of brand-new passion, don't you? You were the voice of reason when we were going all kinds of crazy, remember?"

"Of course I do," Sherri said, smiling. "You were driving yourself crazy trying to pretend like Jared was the wrong man for you when it was perfectly plain that he was the other half of your heart. But you can't say that I saved the day or anything like that. You took a chance on him and trusted your heart and now…" Her voice trailed off and Alexis jumped right in.

"Listen to what you're saying! You're the one who showed me how to trust my heart, you stubborn woman! You're the one who made me make a list of all the qualities I wanted in a mate, and you're the one who made me realize that Jared had all of those qualities and more. True, he's not dark chocolate, but, honey, I have a whole new appreciation for vanilla now," she said as she laughed.

"Alexis, focus, please. It's your turn to be the voice of reason and you're gloating about your sexy husband. You're supposed to be helping me." Her voice was dangerously close to a whine, something that Sherri never, ever did. Now Alexis went into true friend mode.

"Okay, Sherri, let's look at this, umm, objectively," she said. "You're a wonderful woman who has closed herself off from any kind of male companionship because of a disappointing relationship with a worthless man. It happens. It happened to me, too, although we don't talk about it much. I found my fiancé in bed with his ex-girlfriend, remember. I didn't want to be bothered with men either, until Emily and Todd got together and I realized that I really could be happy and in love again."

"Yes, but that was a totally different situation." Sherri had on her stubborn expression, the one that Alexis and Emily knew too well and dreaded. She didn't get that look often, but it always preceded a long and difficult discussion. When Sherri made up her mind about something it was hard to change her point of view. Alexis had to make some good points soon or Sherri would go into her donkey mode, which meant no progress would be made for some time.

"It's not really that different, Sher. Okay, so you weren't looking for a man. You have no list of attributes to compare to Lucas, and you don't think that your night of flaming hot love is the beginning of a serious relationship. I get that, I really do. But you're the only one who thinks that," she said in her most persuasive voice. "Lucas really cares about you. I never said anything to you because I knew you'd flip out, but Jared told me that if you weren't interested in Lucas you'd better run because he recognized the look in his brother's eyes. The look that meant he was going to come after you with all guns blazing because he really wanted you."

Sherri's face underwent a rapid change from wistful

and confused to totally shocked. "He did not. Did he? When did he tell you that?"

Alexis reached over and gave her friend's hand a comforting squeeze. "At our reception, actually. He said that Lucas had the unmistakable look of a VanBuren man who'd found his ideal woman."

"That's crazy talk, Alexis. It doesn't happen like that," she argued.

"Really? Are you forgetting how Jared and I met? He fixed my flat tire on a stormy night and cut his arm while doing it, so I took him to the hospital. The very next evening he came over to take me out, and when he saw me in that red dress we never made it out of the house. Less than twenty-four hours after I met him we were doing things to each other that I didn't know existed and I thought we'd both lost our minds. You were the one who convinced me that his feelings for me were real," she reminded her friend.

"Every time I had doubts you were right there with the reassurance and the insight and common sense and you were absolutely right. So now it's your turn."

"But, Alexis, that was totally different. I could see how he looked at you. I could see the love and affection just shooting out of him every time you two were in the same room."

Alexis was finishing an extra-big piece of cantaloupe, nodding her head vigorously with every word from Sherri. "That's right, sweetheart, and I can see the same thing when Lucas looks at you."

"Lucas calls me sweetheart," Sherri said softly. "It sounds so nice when he says it."

"See? That's what I'm talking about. I know this attraction between you and Lucas wasn't part of your master plan and the whole thing just took you by surprise, but that doesn't mean it isn't real. At least you've known Lucas for several months and you didn't jump his bones right off the bat like I did his brother. You can at least still be considered a woman of virtue—unlike me," she said with a laugh.

"But you've got some thinking to do about this because someone else thinks you're the perfect couple and has already started planning your wedding."

Sherri gave her friend a wary look. "Please tell me you're making that up for dramatic effect. Who on earth could you be talking about?"

Before Alexis could answer, the French doors in the dining room opened and a flurry of fur and little girl invaded the kitchen. "Sookie and Honeybee need some water," Sydney announced.

Sherri obligingly got plastic dishes out and filled them with cold water. As she was doing this, Sydney's eagle eyes noticed the floral tributes from Lucas. "Those are so pretty, Mommy! They're from Uncle Lucas, aren't they?" she asked with obvious enthusiasm. "Can we have flowers like that in your wedding?"

Sherri was in midstoop to place the water-filled dishes in front of the puppies. She was so stunned that she went down on her butt and gave Sydney a dazed look.

"My what?"

"Your wedding to Uncle Lucas. Can we have flowers like that in the wedding?"

Alexis covered her mouth to keep the laughter from exploding out. Sherri covered her eyes.

"Sydney, what makes you think that I'm going to marry Lucas?"

"Because he likes you a lot, Mommy. A whole, whole lot. And he'd make a good husband for you and a daddy for me, and we could all live together and be happy," Sydney said innocently, like it was the most logical thing in the world.

"But, sweetie, that's not the kind of thing that happens just because you want it to," Sherri said gently. "That's something that happens between two people who've known each other for a long time and who care for each other very much. You can't just decide that something is a good idea and hope it happens out of thin air."

"I know that, Mommy. That's why I asked Uncle Lucas if he would marry you. Can I have some cantaloupe?"

Her words were so offhand that Sherri didn't catch on for a moment. "You asked Uncle Lucas if he'd marry me? Why would you do that, Sydney?"

"Because he's so nice and he really likes you, Mommy. He looks at you all the time and he always smiles when he sees you. And you need a nice husband like Auntie Alexis and Auntie Emily have and I need a nice daddy. So I asked him if he would marry you."

"What did Lucas say when you asked him?"

"He said that it had to be your decision and I told him he had to have a plan to get you to want to marry him. He said it was all up to you. I'm hungry, Mommy."

Chapter 9

The weekend couldn't have ended any faster for Sherri. Normally she enjoyed spending time with Sydney more than anything else and she was always a little sad when Monday morning rolled around. It meant that Sherri would be back at work and Sydney would be back in school and there would be five busy days before they would be free to have another weekend adventure. But once Sydney had made it obvious that she expected her mother to marry Lucas, the rest of the weekend was nerve-racking, at least for Sherri. This Monday wasn't tinged with regret that she had to go back to work; today she fully appreciated her tidy office, her efficient staff and the patients waiting to see her because it gave her something else on which to focus her attention. It meant that she had at least eight hours to not think about Lucas.

Sherri was still thinking about her conversation with Sydney while she got ready for her first patient. She had explained to Sydney that marriage was a really big thing between a man and a woman and it wasn't the kind of thing that happened just because someone else thought it was a good idea. She told her that it took a long time for a person to meet the right person to marry and a longer time for them to fall in love. Sydney had listened intently and said, "But it didn't take long for Auntie Alexis and Uncle Jared to love each other. And it didn't take long for Auntie Emily and Uncle Todd. Why can't you fall in love with Uncle Lucas? You like him a lot. I know you do."

Sherri had been dumbfounded at her little girl's insight and logic. "You have the makings of a fine attorney under those braids," she'd told her. "But the bottom line is that marriage is a grown-up thing and you are a little girl. It's not appropriate for you to involve yourself in grown-up situations, especially my grown-up situations. You got that, kiddo?"

Sydney was an obedient child but a persistent one. "But if you get married, I'm involved, too, because your husband would be my daddy, right? So I should be part of it, right?"

Sherri changed tactics slightly because Sydney wasn't giving in yet. "Why have you decided that you want a daddy? I thought we did really well, just the two of us. We live in a nice place, I have a good job, we have really nice friends who love us and treat us like family and you and I have lots of fun. I think our life is pretty good, Sydney."

"It's very good, Mommy," Sydney assured her. "That's why I want Lucas to be in our family, because then it would even better. I have lots of fun with him, Mommy, and so do you. Don't you want to be with him all the time? I do."

After more discussion Sherri was fairly sure that she'd convinced Sydney that while her intentions were pure, her interference was inappropriate and that anything to do with marriage should be left strictly to the adults involved. Sydney said she understood and promised to stay out of her mother's love life. Sherri was, however, dreading her next encounter with Lucas because this time it was bound to be uncomfortable.

She couldn't stop replaying the rest of the weekend like an endless live-feed loop on her mental computer screen. Her mind was occupied as she addressed patients whose asthma treatments needed upgrading or who were recuperating from sprained ankles, measles and other childhood ailments. She forced herself to keep her mind clear and focused on her patients and their parents. It worked wonderfully until it was time for her to take a break for lunch. "Break" was somewhat of a misnomer because she usually stayed in her office and dictated notes on all her patients while she ate something she'd brought from home. When she went to her office, Lucas was waiting for her with a fancy bag from Seven-Seventeen.

Sherri entered the room warily, asking, "Why are you here, Lucas?"

Lucas gave her the easy grin that never failed to melt her heart and said, "I thought I'd bring you lunch and say hello. Come on in. I don't bite unless you want me to."

She straightened her shoulders and walked to the coat hooks behind her desk to hang up her white coat. Sitting down behind her desk, she clasped her hands together before giving him a stern look. "I thought we agreed to take things slowly," she said.

Lucas didn't answer her right away; he was occupied with taking her lunch out of the bag and arranging it on the coffee table in front of the small sofa. "This is slow, Sherri. Believe me, I can move a lot faster," he teased. "Come eat your lunch. You skip too many meals, sweetheart."

There it was again—that tender tone that made her body respond every time she heard it. As if she had no will of her own she rose from the desk and went to the tiny lavatory to wash her hands. When she was finished she seated herself on the sofa and looked at the delicious food. She smiled in spite of any misgivings and thanked Lucas properly.

"This looks wonderful. Thank you so much for doing this. You didn't have to, but I really appreciate it."

"You're more than welcome."

Sherri sighed deeply before turning her attention to the gorgeous spread in front of her. A salad of arugula, romaine and spinach adorned with thin slices of sirloin with marinated artichoke hearts and hearts of palm awaited her. It was garnished with avocado, tomatoes and cucumber and it looked like a magazine cover, right down to the little glass jar that held her favorite dressing, red wine vinaigrette. There was a crusty roll, still warm from the oven, a bunch of tiny champagne grapes and a bottle of green tea. He'd also had the pastry chef from Seven-Seventeen make up a huge box of cookies for her to share with her hardworking staff. Lucas had thought of everything. Sherri spread the cloth napkin he'd provided over her lap before attacking the salad.

After the long, slightly worrisome mother-daughter talk with Sydney, Sherri tried not to fret, but it was impossible. She wasn't a person to act on impulse; the serenity of her life depended on her ability to plan things out calmly and rationally. Her plan had included a life of celibacy until her daughter was safely in college, and she'd neglected the plan. She'd destroyed it totally by going to bed with Lucas and now all these complications had raised their ugly little heads. Sydney thought she was going to marry Lucas and they'd all live happily ever after; right, like that was going to happen. The last thing she wanted to do was see her child hurt by becoming attached to a fantasy that couldn't happen. Somehow she had to get everything back on track, and quickly.

Sherri paused for a moment to look at Lucas. He was so handsome it should have been illegal.

"We need to talk," she said firmly.

"Whatever you wish," Lucas said agreeably.

Lucas sat next to her, so close that she could feel the heat from his body. It distracted her immediately, but things needed to be cleared up right away.

"What's on your mind, sweetheart?"

Hearing that word made something throb deep inside her, and she blurted it out with no finesse at all. "Sydney thinks we should get married and I understand she discussed it with you."

Lucas moved a little closer, his arm thrown casually across the back of the sofa. "Yes, she did. She told me all about it on Mother's Day, as a matter of fact."

"Why didn't you say anything to me? Didn't you think that this was something I should know about? I can't have my child getting all caught up in a fantasy that can't come true, Lucas. That's not fair to her."

Lucas didn't answer for a moment; he was slowly removing the pillow barrier and bringing her closer to his body. "Sydney isn't the kind of kid to indulge in idle fantasy. She's a very smart little girl and very observant, too. She knew I had feelings for you and she knew that you'd be happier with me in your life, so she came to me with a plan. It just so happens that her plan was the same as mine."

Sherri turned so that she was resting against him with her head on his shoulder. She drew her legs up onto the sofa and felt her body relax into his side. His voice was so soothing that it took her a few seconds to register what he'd just said.

"What do you mean her plan was the same as yours? Did you have some kind of agenda in mind, Lucas?"

He lifted her chin so he could take her mouth in one of the long, lingering kisses that made her forget everything but the feel of his lips and the taste of his tongue. When he finally brought the kiss to a satisfying end, he spoke.

"The only agenda I had was to get to know you and to earn your trust and your confidence so that you and I could be a couple. I knew you the first time I met you," he told her.

"You knew me? What does that mean?"

"It means that the men in my family don't mess around. When we meet the woman who's going to be the most important person in our lives, we know her. When I met you at Jared's wedding, I knew," he said simply. "I had planned on taking my time with you and Sydney because I wanted you to trust me and to know that I was the right man for you and the right man to be in your daughter's life. But Miss Sydney kind of jumped the gun." He laughed. "She had everything figured out and she wanted me to step up my game, so I did."

Sherri looked at him carefully, trying to gauge his sincerity. His eyes held nothing but warmth and affection and he looked happy and full of desire for her. She had to be sure, though, of what he was saying.

"And if she hadn't come to you with her crazy idea, what would you have done? What was the outcome supposed to bc, Lucas?" She sounded a little witchy.

"I wouldn't have done anything differently, Sherri. I would have still come after you, no matter how long it took. I would have wooed you, courted you, chased you down or whatever it took to make you mine. I told you, I had the same plan as Sydney—I want to marry you and take care of you and be a father to Sydney. I'm sure it's too soon to tell you all of this, but because all the cards are out on the table, I think you should know what I want so I can see if you want it, too."

The way he'd spoken to her while he was holding her close was too romantic and sexy to recall in such clarity—not while she was in the office. Sherri made her libido go into deep freeze while she hurriedly finished her lunch and took the cookies to the break room for everyone to share. She washed her hands and checked her face to make sure she looked like her usual calm, composed self. Then she put her white coat back on and prepared to meet the rest of her patients for the day. She and Lucas, after a little more conversation and a whole lot more kissing, had agreed to take things slow. They had a plan in place and all they had to do was follow it. Nothing could be easier than that.

Chapter 10

"Lucas, this is so good." Sherri sighed as she licked chocolate from her spoon. Lucas smiled to acknowledge her appreciation. They were eating dessert in her dining room, a delectable finish to the gourmet meal he'd made for her. The meal had been wonderful from beginning to end, but the *pots au chocolat* he'd made were sublime.

"It's always a pleasure to cook for you," Lucas said.

"And I always appreciate it," she told him. "I will clean up to show you how thankful I am that you take the time and make the effort to give me such a lovely meal."

Lucas leaned forward a little and raised one brow. "How many times are we going to have this discussion? You don't clean up around me, babe. I'm here to serve you, so get that through your beautiful head. It will take me ten minutes tops to finish off the kitchen, so why don't you get comfortable and wait for me in the living room?"

It was true; Lucas cleaned as he cooked so that only the dishes they ate from were left when a meal was finished. He really could set everything to rights in mere minutes. Alexis had already warned her that the Van-Buren men were the last of a dying breed of men who took their role as protectors very seriously. In Alexis's words, "They would walk through a wall of fire to protect their women, so she may as well get used to it." It was way too easy to get used to the way Lucas treated her; he was so considerate and caring. Sherri was trying to keep her head about it, but Lucas was winning her heart more and more every day. And now they had a whole week alone.

The school year had ended, leaving Sydney free for the summer. She had summer classes in dance, Vacation Bible School and other programs to participate in while her mother was at work, and Sherri had a vacation planned for them later in the summer. But right now, Sydney was on Hilton Head Island with Lucas's parents. His brother Damon had brought his children down to spend the summer with their grandparents, and the elder VanBurens had invited Sydney to spend a week with them. Sydney was delighted to be included because she loved Lucas's parents and she'd been in Alexis and

Jared's wedding with his niece and nephew. They had become instant friends as a result.

Lucas and Sherri had driven her to Hilton Head and stayed for a few hours while she got settled in. It was nice to see Lucas's brother again; he was outgoing and charming like his twin, and he surprised her with a big hug.

"Welcome to the family, Sherri. I guess I'll have to make more of an effort to get out and meet someone like you since I'm gonna be the last single man standing in the family." He laughed and she laughed with him, but she felt a little shock at his words. He had acted as though her relationship with Lucas was a done deal, something she pointed out to Lucas when they drove back to Columbia.

He just smiled and squeezed the hand that he was holding as he drove. "I'm sorry if he made you uncomfortable, sweetheart. You know that twins share a special bond. He knows what's on my mind and what's in my heart, that's all."

She'd been touched to her own heart by his words, but she didn't say so. Instead she asked him an impulsive question. "Was Damon married? I shouldn't be asking about his personal business, but he has those beautiful children," she said shyly.

Lucas squeezed her hand again. "His best friend was the married one. Damon was godfather to their children and he adopted them when their parents were killed in a boating accident. There was no one else to do it, and he volunteered. He's a great dad. I'm sure you've noticed."

"Yes, I have. And it's not all I've noticed either," she'd murmured.

So now they had a week together without their beloved little chaperone—time to spend together without any restrictions. Sherri was thinking about that very thing when Lucas joined her in the living room. He brought a bottle of wine and two glasses, which he placed on the coffee table before sitting next to her. He put his arm around her shoulders and was pleased when she moved so that she was sitting in his lap. She looped her arms around his neck and leaned closer so she could kiss him. It was a soft, tender caress on the corner of his lips. He could feel the tip of her tongue tease the sensitive spot and he returned the gesture, gently coaxing her lips apart until their mouths were joined.

When the kiss ended, Sherri murmured, "Thank you," before kissing his throat. Lucas's sexy laugh rumbled up from his chest and vibrated his throat against her mouth.

"Why in the world are you thanking me?"

"For making me dinner, for cleaning up afterward, for driving us to Hilton Head, for the fact that you have the sweetest parents in the world who treat my baby like she's one of theirs, for being so patient with me, for just being you," she said quietly. "For everything."

Lucas put one hand on either side of her face and kissed her again. "You don't ever have to thank me for anything, Sherri. You and Sydney are the best things that ever happened to me. I haven't felt anything like what I feel for you in my life," he said, his voice low and intense.

"Is that a good thing?" she teased.

"Let me show you how good," he growled. He placed her so that she was facing him with her legs straddling his body. She moved her hips so she could feel his manhood swelling, getting hard and thick and ready for her. She was wearing a silky little dress with tiny buttons down the front and a flaring skirt that swirled around her legs and allowed him easy access to them. His hands caressed her thighs, moving up and down, loving the feel of her soft, smooth skin.

"You feel so good," he said in a rough whisper.

"You make me feel good," she murmured and moved her hips again. She could feel him, rock-hard and ready.

His hands went to the tiny buttons so he could remove her dress, but she stopped him.

"It doesn't unbutton—those are just for decoration," she whispered. "You have to unzip it. And I have a surprise for you," she added.

Lucas was too aroused to answer; he just put his fingers on the zipper and began to pull it down. When the zipper came all the way down, he slid the delicate fabric off her shoulders, and her surprise was revealed. He grinned when he saw the sheer sexy bra in the soft champagne color.

"No more schoolgirl white." She giggled. "I got an upgrade for you."

She gracefully got off his lap and shimmied the dress down her legs so he could see that she had on a matching thong that showed off everything that made her a woman when she turned to show him her high, rounded derriere. She wiggled her hips to his delight. He got off the sofa at once, picking her up with his hands on her hips. As he lifted her, her legs went around his waist and she gave a throaty laugh that aroused him even more. His mouth came down on hers and they began kissing wildly as Lucas started walking to the stairs. He stopped the kiss long enough to say, "This time I know where to go."

In seconds they were in the bedroom. Lucas placed her on the bed and she turned on a small bedside lamp so they could see each other clearly. He watched her intently as he unbuttoned his linen shirt.

"You are the most beautiful woman I've ever seen," he said reverently.

"Thank you, Lucas. That's very sweet, but I'm pretty average," she said modestly.

He'd removed the rest of his clothing and was looking down at her with desire on his face. "You're crazy," he said roughly as he helped her turn the bed down. He got in the big bed next to her, and the way he looked at her made her blush. She could feel the heat in her cheeks as he examined her like she was a remarkable and priceless work of art.

"You're gorgeous, Sherri. I love your face," he said, kissing her soundly. "You look like a real woman— not like those chicks with the false eyelashes and the crazy hair. You have a real, natural beauty. It shines out of you."

His words were so sweet that Sherri's eyes filled with tears. "No one has ever said that to me before," she whispered.

"That's because you're mine. You were made just for me and I was made for you. No one else had the right to tell you how beautiful and how incredibly sexy you are." She was on her back and he leaned over her, his hand moving up and down her lithe torso. "I love your body. You're slim but strong. And I really love those long pretty legs of yours."

Sherri smiled up at him. "My legs were so skinny and my feet were so big that people used to call me 'the flamingo.' But then I grew into them, I guess. I started running track and they got strong and muscular and I wasn't the flamingo anymore. My feet are still pretty big, though."

They both laughed but Lucas said, "Don't you have a romantic bone in your beautiful body? I'm trying to seduce you, to tell you how much I want you," he pointed out.

She rolled over so that she was on top of him, her legs entwined with his. "I want you just as much, Lucas. And in case you don't know, you're the sexiest man I've ever known. I didn't know what love making was until you. I love the way you look—your height, those shoulders, your cheekbones," she murmured, stroking and kissing him as she counted off his attributes. "I love the way your body feels against mine. The way you touch me drives me crazy." She stopped and rubbed her face against his chest and touched his hand with her fingers.

"When we went to the farmers' market and you helped me out of the car, your hand touched mine and it was like being struck by lightning," she confessed. "I'd never felt anything like it before, and it scared me a little."

"Are you still scared?" he asked.

"Not of you—never in this world."

"That's what I wanted to hear," he murmured. "Now let's see if I can make lightning strike twice."

Sherri raised her body so that she was straddling him and he slipped her bra straps off. She guided his hands to the front fastener and he freed her breasts. He cupped them and flexed his fingers over their soft roundness, circling her sensitive nipples with his thumbs before adjusting his position so that he could fasten his mouth over one. His tongue went over the hardened tip over and over and he sucked on it while squeezing the other one. The sensation drew a passionate response from Sherri; she slid her fingers into his thick, soft hair and held his head in place while her hips began to move against him. She gasped and moaned his name when he moved to the other side and treated her other breast to the same pleasure while his thumb continued to rub the tip.

A delicious pressure was building deep inside her. She was wet and a slow throbbing was taking over; she could feel it coming and she wanted more. Lucas continued to suck her nipples in turn but his hands moved down to her hips. He held her tight with one big warm hand and slid the other one into her, rubbing back and forth and finding her moist and hot, her clit swollen and ready for him. With one quick movement, she was on her back as he removed the tiny thong and his mouth took over. Her legs went over his shoulders and he held her butt in his palms so he could have full access to her essence. His tongue was hot and wet and he devoured her, rolling it around her jewel, stroking it over and over until he felt the throbbing deepen and the juicy flow that let him know she was having her first release.

Her hips were moving wildly, following every stroke of his tongue until the sensations came together in a shattering climax that made her scream his name. He finally let her go, burying his nose in the neatly trimmed cluster of curls at her apex. He moved so that he could join their bodies in one swift stroke, pushing into her sweetness with his name on her lips. She held on to his broad shoulders and he plunged into her taut body, over and over as she ground her hips against him. He could feel his climax approaching and he pulled her up so she could ride him harder until they were both caught by their rising tide of release.

An Important Message from the Publisher

Dear Reader,

Because you've chosen to read one of our fine novels, I'd like to say "thank you"! And, as a special way to say thank you, I'm offering to send you two more Kimani™ Romance novels and two surprise gifts—absolutely FREE! These books will keep it real with true-to-life African American characters that turn up the heat and sizzle with passion.

Please enjoy the free books and gifts with our compliments...

Glenda Howard
For Kimani Press™

Peel off Seal and Place Inside...

K-ROM-13

We'd like to send you two free books to introduce you to Kimani™ Romance books. These novels feature strong, sexy women, and African-American heroes that are charming, loving and true. Our authors fill each page with exceptional dialogue, exciting plot twists, and enough sizzling romance to keep you riveted until the very end!

KIMANI ROMANCE...LOVE'S ULTIMATE DESTINATION

Your two books have a combined cover price of $12.50 in the U.S. or $14.50 in Canada, but are yours **FREE!**

We'll even send you two wonderful surprise gifts. You can't lose!

2 FREE BONUS GIFTS!

We'll send you two wonderful surprise gifts (worth about $10) absolutely FREE just for giving KIMANI™ ROMANCE books a try! Don't miss out—*MAIL THE REPLY CARD TODAY!*

Visit us online at www.ReaderService.com

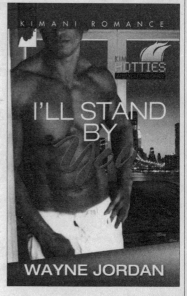

YES! I have placed my Editor's "thank you" Free Gifts seal in the space provided at right. Please send me 2 FREE Books, and my 2 FREE Mystery Gifts. I understand that I am under no obligation to purchase anything further, as explained on the back of this card.

PLACE
FREE GIFTS
SEAL
HERE

168/368 XDL FV2H

Please Print

FIRST NAME

LAST NAME

ADDRESS

APT.#   CITY

STATE/PROV.   ZIP/POSTAL CODE

Thank You!

▲ Detach card and mail today. No stamp needed. ▲

K-KROM-13

♦ HARLEQUIN® READER SERVICE—Here's How It Works:

Accepting your 2 free books and 2 free gifts (gifts valued at approximately $10.00) places you under no obligation to buy anything. You may keep the books and gifts and return the shipping statement marked "cancel." If you do not cancel, about a month later we'll send you 4 additional books and bill you just $4.94 each in the U.S. or $5.49 each in Canada. That is a savings of at least 21% off the cover price. Shipping and handling is just 50¢ per book in the U.S. and 75¢ per book in Canada.* You may cancel at any time, but if you choose to continue, every month we'll send you 4 more books, which you may either purchase at the discount price or return to us and cancel your subscription.

*Terms and prices subject to change without notice. Prices do not include applicable taxes. Sales tax applicable in N.Y. Canadian residents will be charged applicable taxes. Offer not valid in Quebec. All orders subject to credit approval. Credit or debit balances in a customer's account(s) may be offset by any other outstanding balance owed by or to the customer. Offer available while quantities last. Books received may not be as shown. Please allow 4 to 6 weeks for delivery.

They clung to each other, hot, sweaty and totally satisfied, before finally collapsing on the bed. Neither one of them could say a word; they just held each other with the occasional soft, sweet kiss until they fell asleep in each other's arms.

Chapter 11

When Sherri's eyes opened, she was so warm and relaxed that she could have stayed where she was forever. She was lying next to Lucas with both his arms around her, holding her as though he never intended to let her go. Her head was resting on his shoulder and she pressed her mouth to his smooth, tawny skin. He kissed the top of her head in return and she sighed happily.

"That was lovely," she said.

"You're lovely," he corrected her.

"You're sweet. Let's take a shower."

In minutes they were in the shower, their soapy arms locked around each other in a tight embrace as they shared a kiss. Sherri's shower had a teak floor and several showerheads—a huge one directly above the

shower, two handheld ones and several smaller ones that hit the torso area. Lucas insisted on turning them all on, even as Sherri protested.

"I hardly ever use the top one unless I'm shampooing my hair…ooh!"

It was too late; Lucas turned it on and her hair was drenched.

"You so owe me, Lucas VanBuren. I'm going to get you for this," she vowed as she swatted at his hands.

"I'll make it up to you, I promise. In fact, I'll make it up to you right now," he said.

First, he shampooed her hair, loving the way the thick curly strands felt on his fingers. He also lathered Sherri from head to toe, using his hands to excite her while she became pliant and relaxed. Using the handheld shower, he rinsed all the lather away and gave her a mischievous look.

"I have an idea," he said. He moved the teakwood bench until it was directly under the showerhead and had Sherri lie down on it. He adjusted the overhead fixture so that it gave a pulsing spray over her torso. Guiding her so that one leg was on either side of the bench, Lucas knelt down and aimed the handheld shower between her silken thighs. Sherri's eyes opened wide and she giggled from the sensation but the laughter soon turned to moans of satisfaction. Lucas used the various speeds on the handheld to drive her into a frenzy. She loved it. It was a new experience but it was fulfilling, especially when Lucas replaced the shower with his

mouth. She was already aroused by the water play, but when she felt his mouth on her most sensitive spot, her body went wild from the twin sensations of the water beating down on her breasts and Lucas taking her into the stars. Her hips moved in sync with the strokes of his tongue. She felt a shimmering explosion that rocked her so hard her legs locked around him and she cried his name in a shuddering scream.

After a lot more water play, she returned the favor, shampooing his hair and bathing him thoroughly before making him sit on the bench. Now it was her turn to drive him crazy with desire. She took him in her hand and moved her fingers up and down as she circled his broad tip with her tongue, gently squeezing and stroking him while she treated his steel-hard manhood like an ice-cream cone, licking and sucking and exploring every part of him. Now it was Lucas who was calling her name, over and over until he felt like he was breaking into a million pieces.

Soon after, they were back on the bed, wrapped in big, pale green bath sheets. Sherri was fussing at him about the state of her hair, but Lucas didn't see anything wrong with it. She was squeezing the water out of it with a smaller towel, patting it gently. She'd brought a large black jar into the bedroom and when she opened it, a light fragrance filled the room. Using a wooden tongue depressor, she scooped out some of the contents and put it in the palm of one hand. She rubbed her hands together gently before spreading it on her hair

and combing it with a wide-toothed comb. Intrigued, Lucas asked what it was.

"Pure coconut oil," she said. "Haven't you used coconut oil for cooking?"

"I have," he said, examining the jar. "But I've never thought of it as a hair product."

Sherri smiled and said, "It's not just for my hair. I use it all over." She demonstrated by taking some of the oil, which was white, fragrant and solid, and putting it on her arm. It melted immediately and she began to massage it into her skin.

Lucas smiled. "Come over here, sweetheart, and let me do that for you."

He massaged the oil onto every part of her willing body and she did the same to him until they were both bearing the faint gleam of the oil and wearing ridiculously happy smiles. Her hair was almost dry, in a mass of tight ringlets that Lucas thought was sexy as hell. He suddenly remembered the wine he'd left downstairs and asked if she wanted some.

"No. All I want is you," Sherri answered.

"In that case, I'm all yours," he promised. He removed his towel and she took off hers and it was a long time before they thought about wine or anything else but each other.

There was nothing Sherri would've changed about the days and nights she spent with Lucas. She felt closer to him than ever before, which was a revelation in and

of itself. But she also felt calm, happy and relaxed, more than she normally did. Sherri was a very happy person and she had meant it when she told Sydney that the two of them had a great life. She was blessed with a lovable daughter, she had the career she'd worked so hard for and she was able to give her daughter a great life. However, since she and Lucas had become a real couple, she was much happier than she'd been before. She was also physically satisfied in every way, which was another revelation. Until Lucas, she'd had no clue what sex was all about. Now she knew.

She and Lucas spent as much time together as possible, and they took that time to really get to know each other. He was a very open person and really enjoyed talking to her about any and everything. He was also a great listener, and nothing was off-limits for the two of them. She did miss Sydney terribly, but she talked to her every day and she was greatly relieved that she was having the time of her life with the VanBurens. Aside from the strange feeling of not having her precious daughter with her, Sherri's life couldn't have been happier, and it showed.

She came to work singing every day—something she didn't even notice until her nurse, Kayla, pointed it out to her. She had come in early with a big bowl of fruit salad and tiny banana muffins for her staff. She was singing under her breath as she put it in the staff room when Kayla came in with a smile on her pretty face.

"Dr. Sherri, I don't know for sure what's come over you, but it's doing you a world of good," she teased.

Sherri tried to pretend like she didn't know what Kayla meant, but the twinkle in her eyes and her broad smile gave her away.

"Are you saying that I'm usually an ogre to work with?"

"No, Dr. Sherri, you're a great boss. It's just that the past few days you've been extra sparkly or something. It wouldn't have anything to do with that handsome guy that brings you lunch, would it?"

Sherri finished washing her hands at the sink and gave Kayla an extra-mischievous smile as she dried them. "It has everything to do with him, Kayla."

Both women laughed as Sherri went to her office to return calls and get ready for her patients. Her hand was on the phone when her private line rang.

"Dr. Stratton, how may I help you?"

"Where have you been keeping yourself, Sherrilyn? You can't pick up the phone and give your parents a call once in a while?"

Sherri tried hard to keep from making a childish face at the phone, but it was difficult. Her mother, Sybil Stratton, was a difficult person with whom to get along and Sherri had stopped trying to please her years ago. Once her parents found out about her pregnancy they had treated her like a pariah, but Sherri still tried to be a dutiful daughter. After Sydney was born and their attitude actually got worse, Sherri gave up. They had

their lives, and she had hers. She would call maybe once a month to say hello, but that was the extent of their communication. Why Sybil was calling her today was a mystery, one that she hoped would be solved soon.

"Hello, Mother. Is there anything wrong?"

"Of course not. Why would you say something like that?"

"Because you never call me," Sherri said. "What can I do for you today?"

"Well, your father's birthday is on Thursday and we're going out to celebrate. We want you to come."

"Excuse me?"

"I said I want you to come to your father's birthday celebration on Thursday night. So, we'll expect you and your child at the house at eight."

"Mother, thanks for the invitation, but Sydney is on Hilton Head with some friends and I'm not going to get her until Saturday."

"What friends?"

Ignoring her mother's suspicious tone, Sherri said, "What difference does it make to you? She's not going to be there, and I probably won't either. I sent him a card already, so tell him I said happy birthday."

"Sherrilyn, we ask very little of you so I don't see why you can't grant us this little favor and come over on Thursday. You father hasn't been well and I don't know how many birthdays he has left. Ordinarily I wouldn't press, but it's important to him. Can't you see your way clear to act like a daughter and cooperate?"

Sherri wanted to throw the phone across the room, but she refrained. "Fine, Mother, I'll see you Thursday at eight. Is there anything I can bring?"

"Good heavens, no. You know what your cooking does to my digestion. See you Thursday. Please dress appropriately."

Before she could ask her mother what she meant by that, she had hung up. Sherri's lips pressed together in a tight line until she realized she was imitating her mother's standard expression. Whenever Sybil Stratton was annoyed, which was often, her lips would disappear into a line that was so tight, you couldn't stick a needle between them. She shook her head and shrugged her shoulders, shaking off the momentary angst that had arisen from hearing her mother's cool, flat voice. She glanced at her watch and picked up her patient list for the day, putting the phone call completely out of her mind.

She did mention it to Lucas, who looked mildly curious when she mentioned her parents. They were at his loft, relaxing on the sofa and listening to music. He'd made dinner for her again and it was delicious, like everything he prepared.

"You don't talk about them much," he observed.

"My family? No, I don't. There's nothing to talk about, really. We don't have much of a relationship since I disgraced the family by keeping my baby," she said dryly. She looked at Lucas and said, "My people aren't

like yours, Lucas. You have a warm, loving family. They're not afraid to show their love and affection for each other. They like each other. I sometimes wonder why my folks had children because they didn't seem to be too thrilled with us."

"You have siblings? I thought you were an only child."

"No, I have a brother. He moved away after he finished college, and I don't see him often. He lives in D.C. He didn't want to go into the family business, so he was cut off, too," she said, making a noise like a knife going through metal as she dragged her finger across her throat.

Lucas looked shocked, and Sherri put her fingers on his mouth. "Don't say anything, honey. Don't think about my folks. I don't. I'll go and pay my respects, and that'll be the end of it."

She gave him a cheeky smile and continued, "Maybe I'll wear something really tacky and gross like some coochie-cutter shorts and a halter top with platform shoes. Then I'll say, 'Oh, you mean this isn't appropriate?' I'd love to see the look on their faces if I did that!"

"Do you want me to come with you? Because I will, no problem," Lucas offered.

"Absolutely not," Sherri said firmly. "If you meet them, you'll see what a twisted family tree I fell from and you might get scared off."

"Who, me? Never in this world, babe. You may not

realize it yet, but I'm in it for the long haul, sweetheart. I'm not going anywhere except to bed with you."

"Oh, let's do," she murmured. "Let's go right now."

Without a word he scooped Sherri up and headed for the bedroom with her giggling all the way.

Sherri had agreed to make an appearance at her father's party on Thursday, and she went through with it, even though Alexis told her she was crazy. Alexis had a very low opinion of the elder Strattons because of the way they had always treated Sherri. Alexis's mother and Emily's mother had made up for all the maternal loving Sherri didn't get at home, but it was still a sore spot with Alexis. She took being a ride-or-die girlfriend seriously, and she bore grudges like a champ. After all Sherri had been through she didn't see why her friend didn't just cut them off, period, and she said so while she was styling Sherri's hair before the event.

"Just promise me this—if they say anything mean or do anything crazy, get up and get out. Don't say anything—just leave. You don't have to behave like a lady when people are trying to be cruel," she said hotly.

Sherri gave a short laugh. "I promise I will. I'll storm out of there like the devil is on my heels. Wow, I love the hair. You outdid yourself, Lexie. How's my outfit? Is it appropriate?" she asked with a slight twist to her lips.

She was wearing a stylishly cut wrap dress in a deep yellow color that did nice things for her skin color. It had three-quarter-length sleeves and fell to just below

her knees. It was one of the dresses she often wore to
church, and with her usual minimal amount of makeup
and jewelry, she looked stunning.

"You look too good for them," Alexis muttered.
"Come over when the ordeal is finished and tell me
all about it."

"Okay, if it's not too late."

The house in which she'd grown up looked the same
as it always had—austere and forbidding. It was so subdued and quiet that it was like living in one of the family funeral homes. In fact, when she was small, she
thought they did live in a funeral home because it was
decorated in the same style. Heavy satin draperies with
fancy sheer curtains hung at all the windows, and stiff,
uncomfortable brocaded furniture stood at severe right
angles. Dismal-looking landscapes hung on the walls,
and everything seemed to be gray, despite bits of color
here and there.

Sherri parked on the street because it didn't occur
to her to park in the big circular driveway. That was
for her parents and their guests only. She approached
the big gray house with the black trim with slow, mea-
sured steps, then decided she was being ridiculous and
picked up her pace. She rang the doorbell, which seemed
silly because it was her parents' home, but the Strattons
weren't the kind of people you walked in on. So she
rang and waited like a stranger until the door opened.

Sybil Stratton greeted her daughter with a little more

animation than usual, which should have set off alarms in Sherri's head.

"Come in, Sherrilyn. Your father will be pleased to see you. That's an odd color you're wearing, isn't it?"

"Nice to see you, too, Mother. You look well."

Sybil Stratton was a medium woman in every way. She was medium height, medium-sized, medium brown with hair of medium length. There was nothing that stood out about her in any way, but in fairness to her, that was her plan. She wore plain clothes in drab colors because she thought bright colors were vulgar. Standing next to Sherri she looked like a mourning dove beside an oriole. She made no attempt to hug her daughter or shake hands, and Sherri didn't either. She knew the drill by now.

Her mother preceded her into the living room and told her to have a seat, saying that her father would be out in a moment. Sherri looked around in vain for flowers, gifts, decorations or anything to suggest that this was a party, but she found none. She sat on a hard wingback chair and asked her mother how her father was feeling.

"You mentioned that he'd been ill, and I'm concerned about him."

Her mother looked puzzled. "Your father is fine, Sherrilyn. Where did you get the idea that he was ill?"

Before she could state the obvious and say, "from you," her father entered the room. Simon Stratton was tall, lean and quiet by nature. He could have been con-

sidered a handsome man if he dressed with a little more style, but Sybil kept him in dull colors to match hers. He was fair-skinned and freckled, with wire-rimmed glasses, and his thin moustache looked faded with all the gray hairs that populated it.

Sherri rose to greet him and wasn't disappointed when he didn't hug her or show her any kind of affection.

"Happy birthday, Father. You're looking well."

He nodded at her absently. "Hello, Sherrilyn. You haven't changed. I thought you were bringing your daughter."

Your daughter. That's the way they always referred to Sydney. Not *my grandchild, my grandbaby* or anything affectionate; it was always *your daughter.*

Sherri explained again that Sydney was visiting with friends on Hilton Head, wondering as she did it why her mother hadn't explained it to him.

His expression was dour as he said, "That's too bad because there's someone here who wants to meet her."

Sherri was still standing when a tall figure emerged from the dining room. She turned her head to get a good look, and when she did, she was hardly able to speak. Finally she got out a single word: *"Trevor?"*

Chapter 12

Alexis and Jared were entertaining Lucas when the doorbell rang insistently. Jared answered the door to find Sherri on the doorstep, pale as paper.

"What in the world happened?" Alexis asked worriedly. "What did they do to you?"

She hurried across the living room to her friend, but Lucas got there first and put his arm around Sherri. It was obvious that she was upset; she didn't look like herself at all. Lucas could feel her trembling slightly and her breathing was rapid. He led her over to the sofa and sat her down, keeping his arm around her protectively.

"What is it, sweetheart? Can you tell us about it?" His voice was deep with concern.

Jared handed her a glass of ice water, which she took

gratefully and drank in big swallows. "Listen, I'm okay, really. I'm just so damned mad I could spit."

She handed the glass back to Jared with a nice thank-you before leaning back into the comfort of Lucas's arms.

"Jared, you might want to restrain your wife," Sherri warned with a shadow of her usual smile. "I went over to my parents' house for this so-called party and it turned out to be an ambush. Trevor Barnes was there waiting for me."

Jared really did have to put his hands on his lovely wife because she let out a shriek like a steam kettle and jumped up like she was about to take out a gang of zombies single-handed.

"Are you kidding me? Seriously? Where in the hell did they dig him up from, and why was he there?" Alexis sputtered like an angry cat.

Sherri snuggled closer to Lucas just because he felt so good and so warm. "Girl, I can't even give you any details. Everybody's mouth was moving but it all sounded like 'blah, blah, blah' to me. Father said something about me not bringing my daughter with me and I told him she was on Hilton Head with friends. So he said, 'That's too bad, because there's someone here who wants to meet her,' and then Trevor walks out of the dining room."

She shuddered while Alexis continued to fume, letting out a steady stream of vitriol under her breath. Jared managed to sit down with her in his lap and he

asked mildly, "I kind of have an idea, but who is Trevor Barnes?"

"I'll tell you who he is," Alexis began but Jared covered her mouth with his, which calmed her down for the moment.

Sherri's sense of humor came back and she said, "I forget that you're new to the family, Jared, because it seems like you've been around forever. Trevor Barnes is my baby-daddy," she said with a slight snarl. "He was my boyfriend when I was in med school. When I started my internship I found out I was pregnant, I told him and he vanished into thin air."

Jared gave her a long, serious look. "You mean he didn't acknowledge his own child? Does he pay child support, come to visit Sydney, anything?"

"This is the first time I've seen his face or heard his voice since the day I showed him the positive test strip. I was too proud to go chasing after him to make him do right. My parents loved Trevor and wanted me to marry him." She stopped talking when her stomach gave a deep and meaningful growl. "Oh, I'm so sorry! I guess I'm hungry," she said.

"We can't have that. We were just about to eat," Lucas said. "C'mon, tigress, let's get some food into you," he said as he picked Sherri up and carried her toward the kitchen. "Mind if I get the ball rolling?" he asked Alexis and Jared with a smile.

"By all means," Jared responded. "We'll wait here."

Finally she was alone with Lucas. She moved closer

to him, getting into his lap so she could really enjoy the sheer relief of being with him. He held her for a long moment and then kissed her, which made everything okay again.

"I'm sorry for all the drama, honey. I'm usually the levelheaded one. Alexis is the drama queen and Emily is the brilliant one," she said. "But honestly, this is just too much. Can you imagine how I felt walking into my parents' home and finding that louse standing there with a big shit-eating grin on his face?" She giggled and covered her mouth. "I said *shit.* Sorry, I usually don't have to resort to profanity to get a point across."

"Don't you dare apologize for anything, sweetheart. It's a good thing I wasn't there or you would've heard some real cussing—some first-class, prison yard, motorcycle hoodlum cussin'. What was the point of him being there?"

Sherri gave Lucas one more sweet kiss before answering. "Oh, you're going to love this. It seems he's come to town to make amends. He wanted me to know how terribly sorry he is for the horrible, shoddy way he treated me in the past and he especially wants to meet his daughter and become an integral part of her life. Can you believe it?"

She frowned, remembering the ridiculous scene at the house when Trevor came into the living room trying to be all suave. All Sherri could think about was a very old movie called *Blacula;* it was all overemoting and corny dialogue, and Trevor could have played the lead

the way he was going on and on. "Right in front of my parents Trevor started this pompous monologue about his feelings, the error of his ways and the cavernous hole in his heart left by her absence, blah, blah blah."

"What did you say when he started all this baring of his soul?"

"Nothing."

"You didn't say anything at all?"

"Nope. Not a word. I just walked out. I wasn't about to stand there and try to start some kind of meaningful dialogue with the louse, and I was so angry with my parents that I was about to go ziggety-boom, so I left."

Lucas hugged her again, and she sighed with pleasure as she felt his warm loving arms around her.

"Will you come home with me tonight? I have a feeling my phone will be ringing off the hook, and I certainly wouldn't put it past my parents to give him my address. It would be just like him to show up in the middle of the night, and if he does I want you to beat him up."

"I'll be more than happy to beat him until he ropes like okra if he bothers you, but I doubt that he'd be that stupid."

Her stomach growled again, this time so long and loud it was like a sound effect in a horror movie. They both burst out laughing.

"Damn, baby, you got some skillz," he teased.

"Apparently I do. Maybe I can start a new career as a Foley artist or something. I've always been curious

about the movie business. I'm going to wash my hands because something smells really good and I'm obviously weak from hunger."

Lucas helped her rise from his lap and stole one more kiss before she went off to the bathroom. "By the way, you look beautiful in that dress, sweetheart. I love that color against your gorgeous skin."

Her eyes filled up with tears, which alarmed him greatly. "Did I say something wrong?"

"No, you didn't. It was just perfect," she said softly.

While she was washing up, Alexis and Jared came to help in the kitchen. Lucas saw that Alexis had calmed down somewhat, but she was still obviously angry about the dreadful surprise attack on her friend. Jared was putting the finishing touches on the food while she fumed and set places on the work island. She slammed a plate down so hard that it risked being broken into bits.

Lucas straddled a stool and remarked, "I guess you're not a fan of this Trevor person."

"That's way too mild for what I feel about that jackass. I'm also not a big fan of her parents. If you knew what my girl went through, you'd understand why my fondest wish is to douse him in lighter fluid and throw a match at him."

Sherri came into the room just in time to hear this, and she laughed as she stood behind Lucas and wrapped her arms around him. "Don't waste your time thinking about things like that, Lexie. He's not worth it." Her eyes lit up with pure joy when she saw what Jared had

prepared. It was one of her favorite things—pancakes. They were so thick and fluffy that they defied description, and she let out a happy sound of anticipation.

"Jared, thank you. I love pancakes so much and mine never turn out right. These look so good!"

"They taste even better, so hop up there and dig in before they get cold."

She did so at once. They held hands and Lucas said grace, after which she took her first bite of the best pancakes she'd ever eaten. Jared served them with melted butter and some of Alexis's homemade fig preserves with crisply browned sausages on the side. Sherri was in heaven.

"I'm so happy." She sighed. "I go to my parent's house and get waylaid and I come to my best friend's house and get all this love. You didn't have to go to all this trouble for me, Jared, but I thank you from the bottom of my greedy little heart."

Jared leaned over the work island and gave her a kiss on the forehead. "It's never trouble when it's for family, and that's what you are. You're part of our family, Sherri—never forget that."

She could feel tears forming but she forced them back and smiled widely. "Yes, I am," she said as she reached for Lucas's hand and held on for all she was worth.

After an upsetting evening, Sherri's night was much better. She had a delicious, filling meal, the comfort of

her friends and Lucas's love all night long. She was feeling much better the next day, although she knew that there was mischief afoot. To hope that Trevor would slink back to wherever he'd come from was like hoping there was really a Santa Claus.

"I doubt that this Trevor is done with you. He came here to accomplish something, and I don't think he'll leave here until he gets what he wants," Lucas said.

They were in her sunny kitchen, drinking coffee and eating a fluffy omelet, crisp bacon and toast. Sherri agreed with him, but she was much more confident about the situation.

"Like I told you last night—he claims that he wants to make amends and meet his daughter. I have no idea what put the idea in his head. It really doesn't matter because he has nothing coming from me. I'm not too keen on the idea of him meeting Sydney, but we'll cross that bridge when we come to it. Right now, I have to get to work. I'm only in the office this morning and I'm booked solid. I'll be at the hospital all afternoon, and then I have to think of something wonderful to do for you because you were so wonderful to me last night," she said playfully.

"You don't have to do anything but be you," Lucas declared. "Do you want to go out or stay in tonight?"

"Stay in definitely. We're leaving early for Hilton Head, remember?"

"Of course. So why don't you come over to the loft after work and bring your things? I have something in

mind for you," he told her with a seductive gleam in his eyes.

"Sounds just perfect to me. Lucas, you are way too good to me. You know that, right?"

"I know no such thing. I can never be too good to you. You're my heart, Sherri. I'll do anything to make you happy."

The ringing of the phone interrupted the tender moment. Sherri didn't answer it when she saw the call was from her mother. "Okay that's it. That's, what, the fifth time she's called? I'm going to work. I don't have time for drama today."

"Well, you're dressed to handle anything, Dr. Sherri. That color looks great on you."

She smoothed the front of her deep teal sleeveless dress with the mandarin collar. "Thanks, but it'll probably have upchuck or pee on it by the time I get home," she said, laughing. "Sick children have no respect for a power dress. Trust me."

They shared a blazing-hot goodbye kiss at the door and went off to work, Sherri to her office and Lucas to the restaurant. It was a busy, productive morning during which she didn't have to think about Trevor or her parents because she never took personal calls while she was at work. There were several messages waiting for her when she finished with her last patient, though. She sat at the desk and quickly scanned the handful of pink while-you-were-out slips. Her mother had called four times and Trevor had called five times. She rolled her

eyes and tossed them all into the trash. She was going to have to talk to him at some point, but it was going to be on her time and her terms. He just couldn't come to town and expect her to fall all over him, the big jerk.

A knock at the door made her look up. "Come in," she said.

It was Kayla, lugging a huge, gaudy arrangement of blue flowers. Sherri frowned because she knew immediately that these weren't from Lucas.

"Somebody must really be thinking about you, Dr. Sherri," Kayla said with a smile.

Sherri plucked the card from the middle of the arrangement and read it; as she suspected, it was from Trevor. *I can hardly wait to see you. We need to talk,* read the card. Sherri had to bite her tongue to avoid saying something that would shock Kayla. Instead she offered the flowers to her.

"Kayla, didn't you say your mom has a sprained ankle? Maybe these would cheer her up. Why don't you take them to her?"

"She would love them, but are you sure?"

"Absolutely. Give her my best and tell her I hope she feels better soon. Have a good weekend, Kayla."

"You, too, Dr. Sherri. Thanks again for the flowers."

"Don't mention it," Sherri said as she waved goodbye and headed out for her shift at the hospital.

Later that day, Sherri was walking across the hospital parking lot to her car, thinking about a few of her

patients as she approached her Lincoln Navigator. A shadow fell across her as she reached for the door. She gasped and looked up into the face of the man she'd learned to hate.

"Trevor, what are you doing here? How did you even know where I'd be?" she asked with a frown.

Trevor put his hand on his chest in a gesture of contrition. "I didn't mean to scare you, Sherri. Mother Stratton suggested that you might be at the hospital this afternoon and I took a chance. I've called several times and you haven't returned any of them. I went by your office and saw a young woman leaving with a large flower arrangement," he said with a slight edge to his silky tone.

Lovely. So "Mother Stratton" ratted her out to her worst enemy. It was nice to know just how deeply the battle lines were drawn. Sherri was tired from a long day of work and ready for her evening with Lucas. She was short on patience right about then, and her clipped response showed it.

"Trevor, I'm very busy and I don't have time for this. What exactly do you want?"

"I just want to talk to you, Sherri. That's all. I thought I'd expressed myself adequately last night, but because you stormed out I don't think you understand how important this is to me."

"What *this,* Trevor? What could you possibly want from me?"

"I want you back, Sherri. I want you and my daughter back."

Pure rage engulfed her from head to toe. "Seriously, Trevor? Well, that's going to happen when hell freezes over. Now get out of my way before I call security on you."

"Sherri, I think it's in your best interests to listen to what I have to say. After that, I'm sure we can work out an amicable agreement that will be mutually beneficial. Can I have just fifteen minutes of your time?"

"Okay, Trevor, fifteen minutes. No more."

Chapter 13

Sherri led Trevor over to a concrete picnic table under a cluster of trees. She could tell by the look on his face that this wasn't what he had in mind. He could either sit down where the employees took breaks or he could go on his merry way; it didn't make a bit of difference to her. All she wanted to do was find out why he was here in Columbia and what he expected to get from her. He was up to something—of that she had no doubt.

She sat and crossed her arms on the table. She tried with some success to keep the dislike she felt from showing on her face. Trevor hadn't changed much. He was tall, although not as tall as Lucas. His smooth brown skin was the same; of course he still had the same slightly slanted eyes with long straight eyelashes and the

same pouty mouth that she once found so sexy. He had a neatly trimmed goatee in addition to the thick "pornstache" that he affected. It used to make him look dashing, but now it just looked corny. She was pleased to see that his curly black hair was definitely thinning on top. In a few years he'd be good and bald, and it would serve him right. And she was pretty sure that he was toting a bit of a beer belly under his expensive suit. Her lips twitched as she tried to stifle a mean little snicker. Unfortunately, Trevor mistook it for a genuine smile and he immediately began to pile on his version of charm.

"Sherri, I can't tell you how good it is to see you again. You've just blossomed—you really have. You were beautiful when you were in medical school, but now you're just stunning. Stunning," he repeated, as though his evaluation of her looks was somehow paramount to her well-being.

"You have fourteen minutes left, Trevor. Do you really want to waste them on crap talk?" she said coolly. To her amusement he started talking like she'd pushed his fast-forward button.

"I tried to tell you, Sherri, I've realized over the years that I've made a lot of mistakes in my life, but the biggest mistake I ever made was letting you go. I have no excuse for my behavior—none—other than the fact that I was young, scared and stupid," he said, reaching for her hand.

Sherri moved her upper body so that she and her hands were well out of his reach. Trevor hadn't changed

one iota; in one sentence he said he had no excuse, and in the next one he came up with three. She glanced at her watch and tapped it with her forefinger. "Twelve minutes, Trevor."

Hastily, he began again. "I've had a lot of lonely nights to think about what I lost when I ran out on you. Not just your beauty, wit and loving nature, but your intelligence, your ambition. And most important," he said earnestly, leaning forward, "you were the one who cared enough to bring my child into the world. You could have aborted it or given it up for adoption, but you didn't. I'll be on my knees to you in gratitude forever for that."

"Why?"

Trevor looked blank for a moment because he wasn't expecting Sherri to interrupt him. He gamely tried to get his smooth flow going again, but it was useless; she'd thrown him offtrack. Unfortunately, his only comeback was "What?"

"I want to know why you've come back to Columbia to unburden yourself. It's been a long time, Trevor, and all of a sudden you come here and start spouting all this stuff about losing me and your child, a child that you have never even acknowledged in thought, word or deed, and I want to know why. Is this part of a twelve-step program or something?"

"I'm doing this badly, Sherri. I'm not expressing myself the way I want to, probably because this is the most important thing I've ever done. I realize now that I was a

fool to let you go. No woman has ever made me feel the way you did, and I know I'll never feel like that again. I was a fool to abandon you when you told me you were pregnant. I was a total fool. But I want to make it all up to you, Sherri. I want a chance to put things right, to show you that after all the years we spent apart that I've changed. I'm a different man now, and I'm ready to be the kind of man you need. I'm ready to be a real father to my child," he said, his voice choked with the nuanced fervor of a 1950s doo-wop singer.

Sherri glanced at her watch. "Fourteen minutes and twenty-five seconds. Good timing, Trevor. I have to say that I still don't know what you think you accomplished with that speech because I didn't understand what you were trying to say. I've got to go."

She started to rise, but this time Trevor was successful in grasping her hands to stop her.

"What I'm trying to tell you is that I want you back, Sherri. I want to marry you and make a real home for our child. I want you to give me another chance to be the man you deserve," he said with what he thought was passion.

Sherri jerked her hands away and got up from the table so fast that Trevor almost hit his head on the concrete. "Trevor Eugene Barnes, I think you've lost your mind. Do me a favor and stay far away from me from now on."

She was halfway to her car when he caught up with her and grabbed her elbow. "All right, Sherri, all right.

Maybe I'm moving too fast. I can accept that. But I have a right to see my kid. You can't keep her away from me indefinitely and I don't want to have to sue you for visitation, so think about that. And don't keep me waiting too long. I've already waited long enough."

Sherri parked her SUV in front of Lucas's building and took a deep breath. The building had once been a sizable warehouse but it was now loft apartments. Jared had lived here when he first came to Columbia, and he passed it on to Lucas once he and Alexis married. Sherri didn't rush to get out of the car; she needed a few minutes to collect her thoughts.

What kind of craziness was looming in front of her? Trevor had to be on some serious narcotics if he thought that she was going to let him into Sydney's life. All that hoo-ha he'd been talking about wanting her back and wanting to build a life together was too far-fetched to be true. He had to be up to something, and right now she didn't know how to find out what his endgame was.

She finally got her things out of the car and made her way to Lucas's door. She was going to try to put the whole annoying incident out of her mind, at least for a little while. Putting her finger on the bell, she smiled, thinking how good it would be to see Lucas. He always made her feel better no matter what was going on. Sure enough, when he opened the door with his beautiful smile a weight was lifted off her shoulders.

"Hello, sweetheart," he greeted her. She didn't have

a chance to respond before he picked her up and gave her a lingering kiss, right there in the doorway. Finally she was able to speak.

"Hello, yourself. You're looking awfully handsome."

He was wearing an untucked oxford-cloth shirt in a green-blue color that made his eyes look spectacular and a pair of jeans that showed off his long, hard legs and his butt. It had to be against some law for a man to look that good in casual clothes.

She took a deep sniff and grinned. "What smells so good?"

"Something I think you'll really like," he said. He picked up her overnight bag from the hallway and brought it in, scolding her for carrying it. "You should have let me bring your things in, Sherri. You know that's a VanBuren law. No hauling, toting, cleaning or heavy lifting for our ladies."

Sherri didn't pay his words any attention because she was too taken with what she saw in the loft. Candles were lit all around the big living area—on the mantel over the fireplace, in the fireplace, on the dining room table and on the coffee table. It looked beautiful. Besides being full of candlelight, the loft was filled with music. Sherri tilted her head and recognized the distinctive sound of "Mother Nature's Son" by Ramsey Lewis, some of the most seductive jazz in existence.

"Wow," she said in a whisper. "This is amazing, Lucas."

"You haven't seen anything yet. Come with me," he

invited. He took her hand and led her to the bathroom. The big soaking tub was partially filled so it would be ready for her. The big ivory pillar candles were arrayed around the room, and a big fluffy bath sheet was at the ready on a stool by the tub. There was a stand with an ice bucket containing a bottle of green tea and a crystal flute along with a bowl filled with strawberries.

"Lucas, this is the most romantic thing I've ever seen."

"Ahh, we're not done yet," he said, leading her into the bedroom. The bed was freshly made with expensive white linen and big down pillows, and strewn across it was an array of beautiful lingerie—bras and panties and camisoles in delicate colors and patterns, plus a couple of really seductive sheer nighties. Sherri was overcome by his good taste and generosity.

"Lucas, this is too much, honey. These are so beautiful, but there're so many! I can't believe you did this," she murmured.

He gave her a rakish grin and pulled her into his arms for a long hug, followed by an even longer kiss. "Believe it, Sherri. Look, I like the basic schoolgirl white undies—they're as cute as can be. But when I saw you in the fancy ones you looked so damned sexy I wanted you to have more. And if you feel compelled to put on a fashion show for me later, don't hold back," he teased her.

"You'd just love that, wouldn't you?" she said with

a sassy smile. "I will, but only if you do a striptease for me."

"That can be arranged. You know I'm not modest in the least. Listen, you get undressed and relaxed while I finish filling the tub for you. I didn't fill it all the way because I wanted it to be nice and hot."

"You are the most thoughtful man in the world. That sounds like a lovely idea."

"And when you get done, you'll have a fabulous dinner waiting for you." Lucas kissed her on her forehead and then her cheek.

Sherri sighed deeply as she got ready to get in the big tub. Tonight she was just going to take pleasure in the wonderful surprises he had given her, and that was all. The Trevor mess could wait for another day.

After the best bath she'd ever had, Sherri was completely carefree. She rubbed coconut oil all over her body and slipped into a set of her beautiful new underwear, choosing a sheer peach demi-bra with a matching thong. When she emerged from the bedroom wearing a bronze silk tank top and a pair of wide-legged, leopard-print silk pants, she hoped she looked as sexy as she felt. Lucas apparently thought so because he stopped what he was doing in the kitchen to admire her.

"That's a hot outfit, sweetheart. Turn around and let me get a good look."

She did her best imitation of a runway model as she admitted she'd never worn it before. "It was an impulse

buy from T.J.Maxx, and it's really impractical for a working mom of a small child. But I just had to have it. I always hoped I'd have a reason to wear it one day."

"I'm glad you gave in to your impulse because you look fantastic. I'm also glad that I'm the only one to see you in it. If you'll sit down, dinner is served."

He'd made the dining room table look romantic with candles and a single gardenia floating in a bowl of water. The food was delicious, as was everything Lucas prepared, but this was special because it was one of her favorite meals. A first course of pesto-stuffed mushrooms was followed by eggplant parmesan, fettuccini with puttanesca sauce and a green salad with crostini. Sherri was in heaven. Everything was sublime and she told him so several times. He'd even made one of her favorite desserts, tiramisu.

"Lucas, you are too good to me. You're spoiling me something awful," she said, showing her dimples in a beautiful smile.

He scoffed as he poured more wine into their glasses. "You're so sweet that it's a pleasure to do things for you. You deserve it. Anyone who works as hard as you do, and who's raised the world's most adorable little girl, is entitled to be treated like a queen every day of her life."

"Lucas, you're going to make me cry," she warned.

He came around to her side of the table and held out his hand. "Then I'll stop, at least for now. Go in the living room and I'll be back in ten minutes to ravish your body from head to toe."

"Suppose *I* want to ravish *you?*"

"Then I'll be back in five minutes and you can do anything you want to me," he promised.

When Lucas finished in the kitchen he was pleasantly surprised to find that Sherri wasn't in the living room at all. But her sexy leopard-print pants were there, draped over the sofa. The bronze tank top was hanging on the back of a chair and the sheer bra was on the doorknob of the bedroom like an invitation. He entered the room and found Sherri on the bed, bathed in candlelight. She was lying on her side wearing a seductive smile. The thong was dangling from one finger and she was waving it idly from side to side.

"Someone has on too many clothes," she said, her voice a sultry purr.

"I can take care of that," Lucas assured her.

He kicked off his loafers and began to unbutton his shirt with excruciating precision. Sherri sighed in anticipation, but he kept at the buttons, one at a time, as slowly as possible. He finally opened the shirt to reveal his broad golden chest flexing so that his pecs moved one at a time.

"Lucas…" she moaned.

He gave her a wicked smile and said, "You wanted a striptease so I'm giving you what you wanted."

The shirt finally came off and he started on the belt buckle. Once again, he was moving slower than slow, or so it seemed to Sherri. She was already getting wet between her legs, and she could feel her nipples expand-

ing, growing big and hard. Lucas was enjoying her re-action. His movements got more provocative, his hips gyrating and pumping as he inched the belt out of the loops on his jeans.

"If we were in the club I'd be getting some bills," he pointed out.

She rose to her knees and stroked her flat stomach down to her neat patch of curls. Rotating her hips she purred, "I've got your bills right here, big man."

"To hell with this," he muttered, stripping off his jeans and briefs. He joined her on the bed and grabbed her around the waist. "Now what was that about you ravishing me?"

She pushed him back so that he was resting against the pile of pillows at the head of his giant four-poster bed. Her eyes were alight with equal parts desire and mischief as she reached under the pillows and pulled out two silk scarves.

"Do you trust me?"

"You know I do. What are we doing, babe?"

Sherri didn't say anything as she straddled his chest and took one of his hands in hers. She guided it up to the bedpost and tied it loosely with the scarf, then re-peated her action with the other hand. Lucas was smil-ing as she started in on his chest, rubbing the palms of her hands over his flat nipples in a circular pattern. His breathing got harsh as her thumbs began circling his sensitive nipples, making them bullet-hard. One hand

continued its manipulation while her tongue took over on the other side.

She used her tongue and then her teeth to get him ready for more. After she toyed and teased his chest until he was making sounds of satisfaction, she licked her way down his torso to his navel and began kissing it like it was his mouth, circling it with her hot, clever tongue and exploring it until she heard his urgent moaning. She finally relented and kissed her way down to his manhood. Cupping him with one hand and stroking with the other, she tenderly caressed the sensitive tip before using her tongue to tantalize him into submission. Treating him like she would a lollipop, she licked and sucked and tongued until he was trembling and his hips were thrusting wildly. She had no intention of stopping, but Lucas easily freed his hands and took over.

The next thing Sherri knew, she was on her back with her legs apart to take Lucas in as he entered her yearning body. She was more than ready for him, meeting his urgency with the same hot desire. Every time he plunged into her she gripped and squeezed him with her inner walls, pumping harder and harder until he grasped her hips and held her tightly. A deep moan rose from his throat and he pushed again, grinding against her until he couldn't hold back any longer. He let the explosive climax claim him just when Sherri's release came, and their cries mingled in the love-scented glow of the candles.

Chapter 14

Sherri decided to put everything out of her mind except enjoying the day. She and Lucas had a great breakfast and made good time on the drive to Hilton Head to collect Sydney. It was a perfect day with a brilliantly blue sky. She couldn't wait to see her baby. There were very few occasions when Sydney wasn't with her. She had the occasional sleepover with one of her little friends, and sometimes she would spend the night with Alexis, but for the most part, Sherri was a full-time hands-on mom. Having Sydney away for a whole week was a first, and it had had its weird moments. She'd actually gone into Sydney's bedroom on a couple of mornings to wake her up. The feeling that came over her when she looked at the empty bed was hard to bear.

When they arrived at the VanBurens, Sydney ran and jumped into her arms, yelling, "Hi, Mommy!" at the top of her very healthy young lungs. Now they were back together again and everything felt totally right. Sherri got lots of hugs from everyone in the VanBuren family, too. Lucas's parents were effusively glad to see her and hugged her tightly, as did his grandmother.

After they got settled, Delilah couldn't resist making a pithy remark to Sherri. "So you took my advice about my grandson, didn't you? I said you two would make a lovely couple and I was right," she gloated.

Because she was sitting next to Lucas on the old-fashioned glider and he had his arm around her shoulders, there was no point in denying the obvious. Sherri just smiled and tried not to blush. His grandmother was absolutely delighted with the developments and so was Sydney. She was way too young to suss out the intimate details of their new relationship, but she could tell that things were different between her mother and her beloved Uncle Lucas.

Sydney and Courtney, Damon's little girl, watched the two of them carefully all day, and every time Lucas embraced Sherri or gave her a quick kiss, they would giggle madly. Courtney's twin brother, Gabriel, wasn't as intrigued by the spectacle; he didn't see what the big deal was. But Sydney was already deciding what she wanted her dress to look like for the wedding, although she prudently kept that to herself.

Altogether it was a fun day. Sherri brought the Van-

Burens a gift basket of her homemade cookies and brownies along with a nice bottle of wine to thank them for keeping Sydney. Vanessa protested that it was their pleasure, but Sherri could tell the older woman appreciated the gesture.

Lucas and Damon took the children to the farmers' market where they loaded up on fruits and vegetables, and Lucas bought baseball caps for the three children. Then Damon and Lucas made a great lunch for everyone, and Sherri had a great time talking with Jared's parents.

She felt welcomed and well-liked by everyone. It felt like being part of a family, which was a nice way for her to feel. It certainly wasn't like being around her family; there was no judging, no criticizing, no ice-cold indifference and, best of all, everyone here cared for her little girl. While she was mulling this over, Sydney was sitting on Vanessa's lap having her hair rebraided. They were deep in conversation, just like she really was part of their family.

Her parents had always been cool, unemotional people with high expectations for their children, and she and her brother, David, had always exceeded those expectations. They'd both been straight-A students, they both had won full scholarships to college and they were both successful professionals. The one misstep Sherri had in her whole life was thinking that Trevor Barnes loved her. The end result of that liaison was Sydney, a beautiful baby who'd grown into a wonderful child. Her

parents would have had her abort her baby or give it up for adoption rather than appreciate what a joy she was.

And now that louse Trevor had suddenly popped up and said he wanted them back, and her own mother was knee-deep in his twisted plan. *"Mother Stratton" my ass,* she thought angrily, then pushed the angry thoughts away. She was going to keep her mind clear and relaxed until the weekend was over. But when it was over, she was going to lay the law down to Trevor because she didn't want him anywhere around her or her daughter. Never.

When it was time to drive back to Columbia, it was hard to say goodbye to everyone. Sherri's heart was full of gratitude when she saw for herself that her little girl would be dearly missed by everyone. Her eyes got a little misty when Sydney was giving hugs to Delilah and the elder VanBurens. Vanessa was actually teary-eyed.

"I'm going to miss my little Sydney so much, Sherri. You must let her come and spend time with us again. She's such a sweet child. You've raised her to be kind and well-mannered and she's so helpful. You're a wonderful mother, Sherri."

Dr. VanBuren put his arm around his wife's shoulders and leaned down to kiss her on her temple. "You're an exceptional duo, the two of you," he told Sherri. "And Vanessa means every word of what she's saying. We'd love to have Sydney anytime at all. She's part of our family now. She already invited us to her birthday party." He smiled. "I hope that's okay."

"Of course, that would be perfect," Sherri said warmly. "We don't do anything spectacular for birthdays. We usually have a cookout and a birthday cake and that's it, but you're surely welcome. And I know Sydney would love it if Courtney and Gabriel could spend the weekend with us this summer."

After a lot of heartfelt thank-yous from Sherri and Sydney and we'll-miss-yous from the VanBurens, Lucas, Sherri and Sydney headed home. Sydney followed her usual pattern of chattering away like a magpie for the first fifteen minutes or so, then falling sound asleep. Her slumber made it possible for Lucas and Sherri to talk without worrying about her sharp little ears picking up every word. Sherri had warned him that she had ears like a fruit bat.

"I love your family, Lucas."

He smiled and reached for her hand. "They love you, too. And man, are they crazy about Sydney. If you'd let them, they'd be glad to keep her the rest of the summer. But we couldn't be without her for that long—we'd miss her way too much."

Sherri was thinking so hard that she missed his endearing use of the word *we* in talking about Sydney. It just sounded so natural that she didn't pay it any attention. Her mind was full of scattered thoughts, wondering why her own parents were so cold and aloof and what it would have been like to grow up with warmth and closeness the way that Lucas obviously had. And despite her vow to forget about Trevor for the weekend,

she was still curious about why her parents had decided to be his allies and what his ultimate purpose was as far as she and Sydney were concerned. She didn't believe for a minute that he'd suddenly seen the error of his ways and wanted to embrace them into some ready-made family. That was just crazy talk.

She and Lucas talked for a while as he drove to Columbia, but after a while, the soft music and his soothing voice lulled her into sleep. She didn't wake up until he pulled into her driveway. When the SUV came to a stop, her eyes blinked open and she yawned.

"I'm so embarrassed," she said. "I never fall asleep when I'm supposed to be riding shotgun." She sat up hurriedly and rubbed her eyes, unaware that she looked just like Sydney waking from a nap.

Lucas laughed gently. "You weren't supposed to be riding shotgun. You were supposed to be relaxing." He cupped her face with his hand and kissed her deeply. "Why don't you get the door while I get the little one?"

He came around the side of the Rover and opened Sherri's door, helping her down and watching her until she had the front door open. Sydney didn't wake up as he carried her into the condo—not even when he took her upstairs to her bedroom.

"She sleeps like a boulder, doesn't she?" Sherri said fondly. "She always has. Just put her on the bed and I'll wash her up and get her pajamas on."

By the time Lucas had unpacked the Rover and brought everything upstairs, Sherri had Sydney's face

and hands washed, her summer pajamas on and she was all tucked in bed. He couldn't resist giving her a good-night kiss, but she didn't wake up. They went downstairs, and Sherri thanked him again for taking her to Hilton Head.

He walked her over to the sofa and sat down, pulling her into his lap. "Don't be crazy, woman. You never have to thank me for doing anything for you and Sydney."

She put one hand on either side of his face. "Of course I do. It's good manners, for one thing, and for another, I don't want you to think I take you for granted." She punctuated her words with a sweet kiss. Sherri would have been quite content to keep kissing him, but he had other ideas.

"Sweetheart, I didn't say anything earlier, but I think we should discuss it now. What's going on with this Trevor guy?"

She buried her head in his neck and moaned. "Do we have to talk about him right now? Because I really don't want to," she said softly. "I'm tired and you're tired and we're supposed to go to church tomorrow and he's the last thing I want on my mind before I go to sleep."

"You're right," he said softly as he rubbed his cheek against her hair, inhaling her delicate fragrance. "What would you like to think about before you go off to dreamland?"

She turned her face up to him and smiled. "This," she murmured as she parted her lips for his kiss.

* * *

Sherri didn't make it to church after all. She decided to sleep in, and Sydney hopped in bed with her. She got a call from Alexis, who was also giving church a miss that day.

"Listen, do you and Sydney want to meet me at Seven-Seventeen for brunch? Jared and Lucas got this brilliant idea for a Sunday Jazz Brunch and this is its debut. Plus, I'm starving," she said cheerfully.

It sounded like a great idea to Sherri, so she and Sydney got bathed and dressed to meet Alexis. The restaurant was already crowded when they arrived, but Alexis had a nice table in a secluded corner with a big potted palm next to it. It looked as though the brunch was a great success, judging from the number of people lining up for the buffet.

"Where's Uncle Lucas?" Sydney asked.

"He's busy in the kitchen, sweetie. He and Uncle Jared are doing a lot of cooking today," Alexis told her. "Did you have fun with Courtney and Gabriel?"

Sydney's face lit up, and she regaled Alexis with stories of everything she'd done during her visit. Sherri smiled and perused the menu. Every single dish made her mouth water, and she was ready to attack the buffet with her bare hands. A handsome young man wearing the Seven-Seventeen uniform came to their table with milk for Sydney and a pot of coffee for Sherri and Alexis. He smiled as he greeted them.

"Good morning, ladies, and welcome to our first Jazz

Brunch. Chef VanBuren asked me to tell you that a special meal is being prepared for you and will be brought to your table. In the meantime, we'll be serving you a variety of selections from the buffet."

In minutes a pretty server brought them dishes of strawberries and fresh pineapple, piping hot biscuits, creamy grits and shrimp and crisply fried okra. Their first server came back with a passion-fruit Bellini for Sherri and fresh pineapple juice for Sydney and Alexis. Sherri was absolutely in heaven.

"Every time I come here I like it more and more. The food is fantastic and the decor is just beautiful," she said as she looked around the restaurant.

Since its opening, Seven-Seventeen had enjoyed great business. There were many reasons why the place was always busy—the food was delicious and the ambience was soothing yet sophisticated. It was beautifully furnished with dark hardwood floors, slate tiles on the walls, copper wall sconces and rich deep blue walls. There was also a waterfall on the wall in the entrance.

"Camilla, Jared's youngest sister, did the decorating. She does all of their restaurants. Very talented young lady and so sweet. Well, you know, you met her when we got married," Alexis reminded her.

"I remember all of them. They're just the nicest people in the world. His parents and his grandmother were so sweet to Sydney. You married into a great family, Lexie."

A ripple of excitement ran across the room as Lucas,

dressed in his black chef's coat and slacks, walked through the main dining room, greeting guests and chatting with the regulars. He came to their table with his usual charming smile and greeted his sister-in-law and Sydney, and then he bent and gave Sherri a brief but meaningful kiss.

"You look beautiful," he said in a soft voice. "Did you make it to church?"

"No, we slept in because Mommy was tired," Sydney chirped. "Uncle Lucas, can I come see the kitchen with you?"

"Sure you can, honeybun. C'mon and I'll give you the grand tour."

As the two headed off to the kitchen, Alexis was obviously pleased that Sydney was out of earshot. She didn't waste any time in getting down to business with Sherri.

"What's on your mind, sweetie? I can tell you've been entertaining some deep thoughts," she said gently.

"You know me too well," Sherri said, and sighed. "I've been all caught up in this whole Trevor mess. Do you know that he calls my mother 'Mother Stratton'? What's that about? I know that she and Father were all excited when I was dating him and that they blamed me for getting pregnant, but I had no idea that they were still charter members of the Trevor Barnes fan club."

"Good grief. How can they possibly want to be involved with him after what he did to you? And did you ever find out what he's up to? Something rotten must

be afoot for him to come to Columbia and seek you out. He's up to something and it must be no good, the bastard."

Sherri's mouth twitched. "According to Trevor, he's back because he's realized the error of his ways. He wants me back and he wants the three of us to be a family—me, him and Sydney. Can you beat that?"

Alexis's mouth dropped open and her eyes widened. "When did you talk to him?"

"He waylaid me in the parking lot at the hospital on Friday when I was leaving work. 'Mother Stratton' told him where I'd be, and he came looming over me when I was walking to my car. I gave him fifteen minutes to state his case and that's what he came up with. But, Alexis, he said something about wanting to be a part of Sydney's life and not wanting to have to go to court over it, something like that. I was barely listening to him because I was so mad, but I think I should get some legal advice."

She stopped talking long enough to take a healthy swallow of her Bellini before continuing. "I don't see how he can force me to let him have visitation or partial custody—not after the way he's behaved—but nowadays you never know what the court system is going to do in these cases. I hate to admit it, but I'm really concerned about this."

"What did Lucas say when you told him about it?"

Sherri looked sheepish as she stirred her grits. "Nothing."

Alexis was shocked. "Nothing? He didn't give you his support, offer comfort, suggestions, anything?"

Sherri swallowed a forkful of shrimp and grits and dabbed her mouth with her napkin. "He couldn't say anything because I didn't tell him about the parking-lot incident." She raised her hand to forestall the yelp that she expected from Alexis.

"I just didn't want to talk about it then. We were going to Hilton Head to pick up Sydney and I just wanted to enjoy myself, and I did. Everything was so much fun and so peaceful and loving. I would've given anything to have a family like that," she said wistfully.

"You know how my parents are. It was like living in a walk-in freezer. If I hadn't had your mother and Emily's mother to love me I would've grown up to be the most neurotic, needy heifer in South Carolina."

"Instead of being the wonderful woman that you are," Alexis said fiercely. "Just forget about the family dynamic for right now. Let's just concentrate on that fool Trevor. We need to find out what he's up to and fast. I agree—I think you could use some advice from a good attorney because Trevor sounds like he's prepared to be conniving if you don't give him what he wants. I mean, it's not like you're not irresistible, but I'm having a hard time believing that after almost eight years he suddenly decides that you're the love of his life and he has to have you back in his arms—not to mention the child that he's never acknowledged."

She ate with great appetite for a few minutes and then

pointed her fork at Sherri. "Are you going to introduce Sydney to that asshat?"

Sherri's face looked pale and pained. "I don't want to. I really don't. I don't want her to get confused and I certainly don't want her to be hurt, and there's every possibility that this could end badly. But suppose there's some legal ramification for not allowing him access to Sydney? Could that make a judge decide in his favor for custody?"

"Considering the fact that he's never acknowledged his daughter, never tried to communicate with her in any way and never paid a dime in child support, I'd say fat chance of that, but like you said, these days who knows. We need to talk to a lawyer for sure." She took another sip of juice before adding, "And you need to talk to Lucas. He'll be really hurt if you leave him out of the loop."

"You're right," Sherri admitted. "And I will. But you know how I hate drama. His life is so normal, so free of these crazy details, and here I come with a full load of baggage that I didn't even know I had."

Their server came back to the table with plates of big golden waffles and crisply done chicken. They both sighed with anticipation. There was a smaller waffle for Sydney. She came skipping back to the table with Lucas just in time.

"Uncle Lucas made these just for you, Mommy. Aren't they nice?"

Sherri smiled gently as Lucas placed Sydney back in her chair. "The nicest thing ever, sweetie."

"This is the best day, isn't it, Mommy?"

Sherri looked at Sydney and then at Lucas. "Yes, it is. The best day ever." She just hoped that there would be many more after she got Trevor out of their lives once and for all.

Chapter 15

Lucas leaned back in his desk chair and rubbed his face with both hands. He wasn't tired from a long day of work; he was energized, the way he usually was. He had the stamina of a young stallion and it took a lot to make him weary. He felt a weight on his shoulders, however, but it wasn't his. His concern was all for Sherri and Sydney. She'd finally told him about her confrontation with Trevor, and he was proud of the fact that his head hadn't exploded when she did. She had told him Sunday evening after Sydney had been tucked into bed. They had gone downstairs and snuggled up on the sofa. He remembered every word of her confession, if that was what it was.

"I didn't say anything before because I just didn't

want to deal with it. I wanted to get Sydney and have a great weekend and just not deal with the crap. I wasn't scared or anything. I was just angry. The nerve of him, just showing up out of the blue with this crazy idea that we should suddenly be a family after all this time. I couldn't believe the nerve of him. And there are a bunch of holes in his story, Lucas. Like why he's decided all of a sudden that I'm the answer to his prayers or something."

Lucas had listened quietly as she vented her rage over Trevor's sudden appearance in Columbia, but he had a few questions for her.

"So what's your mother's role in this scenario? Was she really close to him or something?"

Sherri's face had darkened, and she frowned. "My parents always loved Trevor. He had finished law school and he'd just started working for a firm here. They just thought he was the best thing that ever happened to me, probably because he came from a wealthy family. They live in L.A. and they're big society people, whatever that means. My parents have always been image-conscious, really concerned about appearance before substance. Father was always worried about what 'people might think'—that was his mantra when we were growing up. And Mother was even more so," she said with a slight roll of her eyes.

"I know he worked hard to make his business successful and I respect him for that, but it always seemed to me that he was more concerned about his public

image than anything else. So was Mother. The way the house looked, the way we were dressed, the way we behaved, all of those things were more important than anything else," she had said sadly.

"Do you know why they were like that? Was it something in their past that made them so status-conscious?"

"I have no idea because strange as it may seem, I don't know that much about how they grew up. Neither one of them will talk about their families much at all. Mother is an only child, and Father has two brothers but they don't live here. They're originally from Virginia, both Mother and Father, and as far as I know neither one of them has been back there since they moved here.

"I have so many questions I don't even know where to begin getting answers. I'm calling my mother tomorrow to find out why she and Father have decided to be on Trevor's side, and I hope she has a good answer because I truly have no clue. You'd think they'd be on my side seeing as how he's the one who ditched me and took off like a jackrabbit when I found out I was pregnant. But they blamed me and my loose behavior for the whole thing. Can you believe it?"

"No, I really can't. I can't imagine my parents acting like that toward my sisters. In fact, I can guarantee you they would have had the opposite reaction."

"Yes, well my parents have always been the way they are—very cool and lacking in emotion. Tomorrow I'm going to pin Mother down for some answers and we'll see how unemotional she is then," Sherri had said

grimly. "But as curious as I am about her role in this, I have bigger things to deal with. Like why has Trevor decided that he wants to be a part of Sydney's life? I don't even know if I should introduce him to her, but he made it seem like he'd go through legal channels if I don't."

Lucas had had to work hard to contain himself once he'd heard that. "Don't do it, Sherri. I don't know much about the law, but after the way he's behaved I doubt that he has a leg to stand on as far as any kind of custody is concerned. Have you thought about talking to an attorney?"

"Of course I have. I have an appointment tomorrow with an excellent guy who specializes in family law and custody issues. Sydney's well-being is my first and foremost concern. I have to protect her above all else," she had said fiercely. "I don't want her to be hurt by whatever craziness Trevor has cooked up in his head." She then had sighed deeply and put her head on his shoulder. "What a mess."

Lucas had just held her for a few minutes, but he had to make a point. "Sherri, sweetheart, I wish you'd talked to me sooner," he had said gently. "That's what I'm here for—to listen to you and to give you support and whatever else you need."

"I didn't want to bother you with my problems, Lucas. I'm used to handling things on my own."

"I'm not trying to say that you can't handle your business. You're one of the most capable people I've ever met in my life. You put yourself through med school,

and you raised an astounding child while you were doing it. Now you have a successful practice and the greatest little girl in the world, so nobody can say you're not capable. But what's the point of having a man if you can't confide in him and lean on him once in a while?"

Sherri had gone so silent that Lucas was afraid he'd said something terribly wrong, but then she'd looked up at him with a sweet smile.

"So you're my man?"

"Of course I am, and you're my woman. I think we're too old to be boyfriend and girlfriend, but I was under the distinct impression that I mean something to you. You mean everything to me, you and Miss Sydney."

"You mean a lot to us, too, Lucas. Sydney's crazy about you and so am I," she had confessed. "I've never felt like this about anyone else."

"That's good to know because I was hoping that I wasn't the only one who'd fallen in love. You know I love you, right?"

She'd given him a mischievous smile and said, "I thought you might like me a whole lot, but I didn't want to assume anything."

He had kissed her hard and long to shut off her merry laughter and when the kiss had ended, he'd told her, "Just assume this—as long as I'm breathing I'm not going to let anything happen to you or Sydney and that includes anything that jackass Barnes has up his sleeve. So just put him out of your mind, okay?"

"If only it were that easy," she had said with a sigh.

Then she'd kissed him, and they didn't talk about anything else for a while.

As Lucas recalled that conversation, he was very happy with parts of it, but he was still troubled by Trevor Barnes. He needed to know what the sleazebag was up to and fast. He glanced at the clock on his desk, calculating that Sherri was having her showdown with her mother right about now, which gave him time to check in with a man who was the most reliable source of information about any and everyone in the world. If he couldn't get to the bottom of the Trevor Barnes mystery, no one could.

Sherri turned off her engine and glanced at the back door of Stratton's Funeral Home. She wasn't impressed by the appearance of the building at all, even though it was, like all of the locations, in superb condition. It was basic brick, painted white with gray trim, very plain and austere but with the dignity that was appropriate to an establishment of its kind. The lawn was perfectly green, the shrubs were meticulously trimmed and the sidewalks were cleaner than some people's floors. Even the parking lot was devoid of so much as a leaf or scrap of paper. With a brief sigh she got out of the SUV and walked to the door. She knew her mother was there because her schedule was maintained so rigidly that nothing would have kept her from being at her desk.

After entering the building with her key, Sherri blinked to accustom her eyes to the dim lighting after

being in the bright sunlight. She walked down the familiar hallway to her mother's office, knocking politely on the door. Even though the door was open, she knew better than to invade her mother's privacy without permission.

Sybil looked up from her paperwork with mild surprise on her face. "What are you doing here, Sherrilyn? I don't remember making an appointment with you today."

An appointment to see her own child—how sad. Sherri ignored that and took one of the chairs in front of the desk.

"No, Mother, we don't have an appointment, but there are some things that need to be discussed and that's why I'm here. I won't take up too much of your time—I just want to know what's going on with you and Trevor. Why did he show up here in Columbia after all this time, and why are you suddenly so close to him that he calls you 'Mother Stratton'? I think I'm entitled to some answers and I know you're the one who can provide them." She crossed her legs at the ankle and waited for a reply, which came immediately.

"Sherrilyn, I don't appreciate you barging in here interrogating me like I'm a criminal. You're acting as though something underhanded is going on when you should be grateful that Trevor has realized that he's still in love with you and wants to be a father to your child. He called us a few weeks ago and told us that he was coming to town to ask for your hand in marriage and

we were thrilled to hear it. It's about time that something was done to legitimize your situation," she said with a self-righteous sniff.

Sherri's temper flared. She had to exercise a great deal of control not to let it get the best of her. "Legitimize what situation? Mother, I'm a doctor, for heaven's sake. I have a child and no husband, and so what? That doesn't stop me from being a decent member of society and it certainly doesn't make my baby some kind of social pariah. You act like this is ninety-fifty something instead of 2013. I'm educated, employed and respected by everyone in Columbia except you and my father," she said hotly.

"You're so ashamed of me and Sydney that when you get a call from the creep who deserted me almost eight years ago that you start jumping through hoops because he's suddenly decided that he wants to put a ring on it. I always knew that you and Father cared more about your businesses than your children, but this is too much, even for you."

Her mother's face quivered for a second before freezing into its usual unexpressive mask. "It wasn't always so easy for a woman to have a child out of wedlock," she said slowly. "It was the end of her and any aspirations she might have had for her future. She was turned out by her family and shunned by any decent people because an illegitimate child was a disgrace."

Sherri's faced flamed with anger. "My baby isn't a disgrace—she's my joy. If you ever spent any real time

with her you'd know what she's like. Sydney is a beautiful gift—she's not some burden. If you only knew how much I love being her mother, how fortunate I am, you'd change your tune. You sound like you were born in another century, Mother. It's been a long time since the unwed mother was run out of town."

"It wasn't that long ago," her mother replied. "I hadn't been dating your father that long before we found out that I was carrying you. I had to leave college because it was against the rules for someone like me to attend. I lost my scholarship. My parents forced me to marry your father even though we weren't really in love. We were just wild and stupid and full of sin," she said, bitterness filling her voice.

"I had planned on being a teacher and traveling the world in the summer when school was out. I had a whole life planned that didn't involve a husband or children. And what I got was an unpaid job in a funeral home and two children to take care of. When John's parents found out what we'd done, he was cut off from the family. They own an insurance company with branches all over the world, and he should be getting his share of the profits instead of taking care of dead people. So here we are, living a life neither of us wanted and you have the nerve to tell me that getting pregnant out of wedlock doesn't carry any consequences. It does, Sherrilyn. It will haunt you to the day you die."

Her mother's face was pale and pasty with perspiration trickling down. Sherri had never seen her look-

ing so wrought up. She went to the dispenser in the corner of the room and filled a paper cup with cold water. Her mother brushed it away but Sherri insisted that she take it.

"This is why I was so happy when Trevor called," her mother went on. "This way you can erase the stain on your child by marrying her father. You don't want to have one of those marriages where all the children look like strangers. If you marry somebody else and have another child, God knows what it will look like. Now all your children will look alike and nobody can say that your child is a bastard because you and her father will be husband and wife under God. Don't you see that this is the best answer for everyone?"

Sherri sat down heavily in the chair she'd vacated. "What I see is that you've had way too much time to think about this, Mother. You should have gotten counseling instead of letting all this fester inside you for all these years. I always wondered what made you tick, and now I know. You've always blamed me for everything that went wrong in your life, haven't you? And when I got pregnant and didn't burst into flames, it pissed you off, didn't it? You were furious because I was able to keep pushing and finish my education and fulfill my ambitions and that's why you always treated Sydney like a stray puppy that wandered into your yard." She shook her head slowly as she rose from the chair.

"Well, you don't have to worry about either of us

anymore, Mother Stratton, because I'm done." She picked up her purse and walked out of the office, never turning back.

Chapter 16

By the time she got home, Sherri was exhausted. She'd stopped by the church daycare center to pick up Sydney, and they decided to pick up a rotisserie chicken and a salad for dinner, with ice cream for dessert. Sydney was in her usual bubbly mood and Sherri was glad to see her that way. She was still angry about the scene with her mother, although a part of her felt sorry for the woman. No wonder she'd been such a cold, empty shell of a mother, Sherri thought.

Sydney went off to hang up her backpack and wash her hands so she could help with dinner and Sherri went to the kitchen to put away the few groceries she'd bought. Her mind was still racing when her cell phone rang. It was Lucas, which made her smile.

"What are you ladies doing for dinner?" he wanted to know.

"We picked up a rotisserie chicken and some salad," she replied. "Want to join us?"

"I'd love to," he said. "But why don't you hold the chicken until tomorrow and I'll bring dinner? I'll see you in about fifteen minutes, okay?"

After the call ended, Sherri let Sydney know about their change in plans, and she was thrilled to be seeing Lucas, as usual. They went out on the deck to water their flowering plants and the small plot of strawberries they were carefully growing. When Lucas arrived, Sydney was so excited that she ran through the condo leaving muddy footprints all the way. Sherri laughed as she got out the mop to clean it up.

"Lucas, make her take those shoes off and leave them on the mat," she called when she heard his voice.

She was finishing the mopping when he entered the kitchen and he grabbed her around the waist for a kiss. Everything felt so warm and homey that she was touched to her heart. This was normal; this was like being in a family, with or without "legitimization" or whatever strange word her mother had used. Despite the afternoon's ordeal, she felt happy just being with Sydney and Lucas.

Dinner was fun and festive, even on such short notice. She and Sydney set the table while Lucas got the food into serving dishes. Colorful napkins set off the white plates, and fat candles lent the room a nice glow.

Lucas had brought them a caprese salad with mozzarella he'd made at the restaurant, plus broccoli rabe and the most astounding ravioli she'd ever eaten. It was hand-made pasta stuffed with well-seasoned roast chicken and covered with a brown-butter and sage sauce that made her want to lick her plate. Sydney ate every bite, impressing Lucas once again with her appetite. He commented on it to Sherri, who nodded her head with a smile.

"She's always been a very good eater. She was never terribly interested in baby food actually. Whatever I was eating, that's what she wanted. I used to have to make her food myself because I basically had to grind up regular food for her. Once she got enough teeth, though, it was on and poppin'," she said with a laugh. "If you want to insult her, show her a kiddie menu. She wouldn't eat a chicken nugget if you paid her. She likes really good food—always has."

While Lucas cleaned up the kitchen, Sherri went upstairs to give Sydney her bath. Sydney was very happy about the evening's impromptu meal with Lucas. She splashed around in the bathtub and talked about it while Sherri washed her back.

"Mommy, this was so much fun, wasn't it? I love Uncle Lucas."

"Yes, it was a lot of fun, sweetie. Uncle Lucas loves you, too."

"We could do this every night if you married him," Sydney said guilelessly.

"Hmm" was all Sherri would say. They finished the bath and Sherri wrapped her up in a big towel.

"Go put on your pajamas and you can come downstairs for some dessert. How's that?"

"Okay, Mommy!"

Sherri tidied the bathroom and went down to the kitchen to find Lucas making a salad from the chicken. It looked delicious, full of celery, red grapes and toasted pecans.

"Wow, that's pretty. I love chicken salad. If I wasn't so full from that spectacular meal I'd eat some now. You're so good to me, Lucas."

She stood behind him and put her arms around his waist. He turned around and draped his arms over her shoulder for a kiss, which was how Sydney discovered them when she skipped into the room.

Sherri pulled away from him but he was reluctant to let her go. Sydney reacted with her usual aplomb. "Everybody kisses, Mommy. Uncle Jared and Auntie Alexis kiss a whole lot. You should kiss Uncle Lucas more. It'll make you happy. What's for dessert?"

Lucas laughed heartily while Sherri mumbled, "Out of the mouths of babes," as she went to the refrigerator to get the ice cream and sliced strawberries.

Later, after Sydney was tucked in bed by both of them, Sherri told Lucas about the scene with her mother. He was lying on the sofa with a pile of throw pillows behind him and she was on top of him, her legs between

his. She was so relaxed and comfortable she could have drifted off to sleep in his arms, but she had to tell him what she'd discovered about her mother. It didn't take her very long to relate the whole story.

"Wow," he said when she finished. "That's some story."

"The sad thing is, it's not that unusual," she said. "How many women have found themselves in that situation? And how many of them have just kept on pushing to get what they wanted in life? Part of me feels bad for her because it's obvious that she still feels a lot of hurt for what happened and the way it happened. But part of me wants to tell her to suck it up," she admitted.

"She had a choice. Maybe not in what happened— her getting kicked out of school and losing her scholarship. I mean, things were very different then. But she had a choice in what happened afterward. If she wanted to go back to school, she could have found a way. If she wanted this other life, she could have figured out a way to make it happen. Instead she went through life in a marriage she didn't want with a child she blamed for everything. It's really sad."

Lucas held her and kissed the top of her head as his fingers played in the soft hair at the nape of her neck. "So she really doesn't know why Trevor suddenly shows up to claim you and Sydney, does she?"

"Nope, and she couldn't care less. It never occurred to her to ask. She's so happy that someone is offering to dip me in the pool of holy matrimony and make me

pure again she's not asking any questions. But I want to know what he's up to, Lucas. I don't trust him any further than I can throw an elephant, and I don't want him anywhere around Sydney until I know what his endgame is."

"What did the lawyer say to do about it?"

"I didn't get to talk to him today. He was in a deposition or something, so I'll see him tomorrow. It's just as well," she said with a delicate yawn. "I've had all the info I could handle today."

"You're getting sleepy," Lucas observed.

"Yes, but you feel so good," she murmured.

"I'm going to let you go to bed," he said. "I might have some news for you tomorrow. I have a friend who's an investigator and I had him start digging into Trevor's life. There's bound to be something out there that he can find out about the timing of his sudden desire to have you and Sydney back in his life."

"That would be really helpful, Lucas. You're way too good to me."

He put his hand under her chin and tilted her face up to his. He kissed her with great tenderness. "You're going to have to get used to it, sweetheart. You deserve all the TLC in the world and I plan to give it to you and Sydney as often as I can, so relax. I got this, babe."

"Anything you say," she said sleepily. "Anything at all."

Sherri didn't know what to expect when she went to the law office of Royce Griffin. She'd never met

him; he was recommended by Alexis's mother, Aretha Sharp. Aretha had worked with him on many committees and had turned to him countless times on behalf of people in the community who needed top-notch legal services but had very little money. Royce was a legal legend in South Carolina, and he never turned anyone away, regardless of their ability to pay. The office was in a part of town that had seen better days. It was the exact opposite of luxurious, but the building was clean and cared for.

She opened his office door and found the reception area immaculately clean, although the furnishings weren't new. There were large plants, two sofas and several chairs, none of which matched, but all of them were in good repair and looked comfortable. A birdcage containing a large parrot was on a stand in the corner. As soon as the bird laid eyes on her it squawked and then said, "Client! Client! Get out here—client!"

Sherri's eyes widened and she laughed as a door opened and a tall, broad-shouldered man came to greet her.

"Sorry about that," he said in a pleasant voice. "My secretary is at lunch and Thelonius is better than an intercom, so we put up with him."

Thelonius squawked again. "Damned right you do."

Royce chuckled and escorted Sherri into his office. "He was payment for a case I did a few years ago. Unfortunately, he has a vocabulary of profanity like a drunken sailor on port day, so let's go in here and get

a little privacy." He offered her a seat and extended his hand to shake. "I'm Royce Griffin, and I'm guessing you're Dr. Stratton."

She shook his hand, saying, "Call me Sherri, please." If the matter hadn't been so serious, she'd have taken a minute or sixty just to stare at him. Royce Griffin was seriously handsome in an exotic way. He had it all—height, broad shoulders, beautiful bronze skin, thick and slightly wavy black hair in a long ponytail and high cheekbones with an aquiline nose. His thick brows slashed over eyes that had a slight upward slant and his lips looked chiseled out of copper. He was obviously a mix of several races and the blend yielded a perfect specimen of man. He was nattily attired in a pair of dress slacks and a pale blue oxford-cloth shirt that strained a little over those big shoulders. His neat appearance was at odds with his office; it was the only presentable area of the office.

The walls were lined with books, as expected in an attorney's office. The usual diplomas and honors were displayed on one wall. The rest was chaos as far as she could see. Files were stacked on every flat surface, even the floor. They were neat stacks, but they were everywhere. The remains of his lunch were on a computer desk near the window, and the wastepaper basket was overflowing. She was trying to take everything in when he offered an explanation.

"I'm sure this isn't what you were expecting in a law office, but in my defense, I can find everything I need

at a moment's notice. I have a photographic memory and it serves me well, but it drives everyone else around me crazy, especially my secretary. So don't pay all this any attention. I can assure you that you'll get the best legal advice in the state from me. I'm not bragging— it's a fact. And if you're not satisfied, there's no charge. Aretha asked me to give you my best and there's no way I'd ever disappoint her. She's a wonderful woman," he said, "and someone I hold in very high esteem, so I'm all yours. Tell me about your situation."

Sherri felt compelled to trust him, unorthodox as his approach might be. She gave it to him as concisely as possible without leaving anything out. She explained how she'd found herself pregnant after dating Sydney's father for two years, how he decamped for California as soon as she revealed her condition and how she'd never heard from him again until the day she'd encountered him at her parents' house.

"What I don't understand is why he's decided to come here and try to get me to marry him out of the blue. He's never shown the least bit of concern over his child. To be honest I don't think he knew whether he fathered a son or a daughter. Now he wants to not only make amends, but he also wants to marry me and he wants us to be a family," she said with a frown.

"I have no reason whatsoever to trust him or his motives. I don't want him anywhere around my daughter until I know what he's up to. My primary concern is Sydney. I can take care of myself, but her welfare is my

biggest concern. He's being really subtle about it, but he did say something along the lines of 'I'd hate to take you to court.' And because he's an attorney, there's no telling what he could do in court. Do I have to allow him to meet her? Is there a way that I can keep him out of her life, or will doing so backfire on me when or if we end up going to court for some kind of custody arrangement?"

She finally stopped talking and apologized. "I'm sorry that I just ran off at the mouth like that, but it all came up out of nowhere and it's not going to go away just because I want it to." She took a deep breath and accepted the glass of icy-cold water he poured her from a carafe on his windowsill.

Royce's voice was soft and comforting and his words were even more so. "Look, at this point I really don't think you have anything to worry about as far as him being able to get custody, not even visitation. Has he ever tried to establish paternity?"

"No. He left Columbia as soon as I told him the test was positive, and as far as I know, he never looked back. He was my only sexual partner and he has to know that Sydney is his child, even though I didn't put his name on her birth certificate."

"Did you ever try to contact him regarding child support?"

"I was too angry and too proud. I never asked him for a dime, even though it would've made our lives easier, at least when I was doing my internship and residency.

If he didn't want us, we didn't want him," she said with a touch of defiance.

"Man, he was a big fool," Royce said with admiration in his voice. "Do you have a man in your life right now?"

She blushed becomingly at the sudden turn in his questions. "Yes, I do."

"Sorry, I couldn't resist," he said with a self-deprecating grin. "I'm human—what can I say? Back to business. First of all, unless he's willing and able to come up with seven years of child support in one lump sum, you don't have to worry about visitation at this point. The fact that he's been so cavalier about the existence of his child for all this time doesn't make him a candidate for father of the year. Very few judges would be willing to entertain the idea of allowing him into her life until he shows the willingness and ability to act as a responsible parent—something you've done all by yourself for all these years."

Sherri was immediately comforted by his assessment of the situation.

"In fact, I'd keep them as far apart as possible until we determine what he has to gain by claiming her. There has to be something in it for him and we have to uncover his motive. Beautiful and brilliant as you are, the notion that he suddenly woke from a deep sleep to decide that you're his soul mate is more than a little shaky. So let's find out what his real motivation is, shall we?"

He cleared a space on his crowded desk and whipped out a legal pad and a pen. "Okay, let's start with the basics. What's his name?"

"Trevor Barnes," she answered.

Royce's eyes went from the legal pad to lock onto hers with a look of disbelief. "You've got to be kidding. Trevor Barnes? Did he go to law school at University of South Carolina?"

"Yes, he did," Sherri said with confusion on her face. "We met when he was in school."

"Is he tall, brown-skinned with curly black hair, used to drive a silver Mercedes?"

"Yes, he did. I'd forgotten about that car, but he really loved it."

"We were in the same year at USC. May I say that you had a very narrow escape, Sherri? If he'd stepped up and done the right thing by staying with you, your life would be hell right about now. Did he ever pass the bar exam?"

"Of course he did. He passed it before he left Columbia. That's one of the reasons he bailed because he'd just gotten a job with this…" Her voice trailed off because Royce was shaking his head back and forth with his eyes shut.

"Trevor Barnes was in the bottom tenth of our class. He was nowhere near passing the bar exam when he was here, and he had no job offers whatsoever, unless some firm needed a janitor. As a matter of fact, word around the campfire is that he still hasn't managed to

pass the bar. I stay in touch with a lot of the people I went to school with, especially my frat brothers. It's like a running joke among us that he still hasn't made it. The last I heard, he has a job selling high-end used cars in Pomona or someplace like that."

Sherri's mouth dropped open and her eyes were like saucers, but Royce wasn't finished.

"This is all making more sense now that I know that the man in question is my old classmate. I don't know if you're aware of this or not, but Trevor's family is loaded. His grandfather is a self-made millionaire, maybe a billionaire. He made his money the old-fashioned way— he earned it. He was a pharmacist who developed a lot of medicines that he patented and ended up owning a huge pharmaceutical company. His son, Trevor's father, didn't have the gene for scientific research, but he has a brilliant legal mind, so he helped keep the company in the family's hands. They've staved off every take-over attempt and kept it private, even though they've had all kinds of offers to go public," Royce explained.

Fascinated by what she was hearing, Sherri asked how Royce knew all of the family history.

"Because Trevor couldn't stop bragging about it— that's how. He was my fraternity brother and we shared a house with some other guys for a while. Didn't he talk to you about his brilliant future as the scion of Barnes Pharmaceuticals? Didn't you notice how much money he had? He wasn't the typical starving law student, not by a long shot."

"Are you serious? I know I sound really stupid here, but I don't remember Trevor flashing any money around me. The only thing he had of value was his car, and he said it was a gift for graduating at the top of his class when he got his bachelor's. He never seemed to have any money, not that I really paid any attention. Med school is pretty all-consuming. It's a miracle that I had any time to spend with him," she said.

She was deep in thought for a moment, trying to remember details of their dating life. "He talked about his family from time to time, but I honestly don't remember him talking about money per se," she admitted. "I had the impression that they were well-to-do, I guess, but frankly, that's not a big interest of mine. I was really naive, wasn't I?"

Royce assured her that she wasn't. "You were a hardworking, serious student. Trevor was used to the flashy chicks who were after a rich guy, so you were probably a whole new world for him. But be that as it may, I've got the feeling that his sudden epiphany about you being the love of his life has something to do with his family's money. Let me make a few phone calls and I'll see what I can find out. It won't be too hard because, as I said, I've stayed in touch with our line brothers and I've got a kind of pipeline of chatter that I can tap.

"In the meantime, just keep to the status quo. If he contacts you again, and he will, let me know immediately. If he threatens you with any legal action, refer him to your attorney—that's me. And by all means, keep

him away from Sydney. He hasn't earned the right to be around her and I agree that it's only going to cause turmoil if he gets near her."

They talked about a few other details, and as Sherri got ready to leave his office she was feeling much better. Of all the lawyers in Columbia, she'd been steered to the right one, thanks to Aretha Sharp. What were the odds of her going to see someone who actually knew Trevor from law school? There was a light at the end of the tunnel after all, and its name was Royce Griffin. She couldn't wait to share her news with Lucas. As Royce escorted her to the door, Thelonius ruffled his feathers and said, "See you soon, pretty lady," which made her burst out laughing. It was the perfect note on which to end her first conference. Everything was going to be fine. She knew it now.

Chapter 17

Sherri's feeling of optimism lasted as long as it took her to drive home from Royce's office to pick up Sydney's dance bag. She'd been so preoccupied with her impending appointment that she'd forgotten it when they left for daycare, so she made a quick run to pick up the bag and drop it off at daycare so that Sydney could have it when it was time for her class that afternoon. She parked in the driveway, ran inside and grabbed the bag from the foyer, but when she turned to go back to the car, there was Trevor. He had on a blue suit and was carrying another bouquet of blue flowers. He also had a smug smile on his face. She tightened her grip on the handles of the small duffel bag.

"Make this the last time you violate my privacy or

there will be a restraining order sworn out on you," she said in a cold and even tone. "I've made it abundantly clear that I don't wish to have anything to do with you, yet you persist in accosting me. It has to stop."

The smug smile shifted to an icy smirk so quickly that most people would have missed the transition, but Sherri saw it at once. In a second he went from looking annoying to looking predatory.

"You're using some rather inflammatory terms to describe a harmless social call, Sherri. Violate? Accost? I came to say hello and to bring you something to brighten your day, and you're acting as though I'm a common criminal. Is that any way to treat your future husband?" He had the colossal nerve to try for a winsome grin, as if that would win her over.

"Trevor, I have no intention of marrying you, now or ever. You were not invited here and if you are unexpected, you are also uninvited, so you need to leave. And those things couldn't possibly brighten my day. You've forgotten that I despise cut flowers, and I particularly hate blue ones, so this has been a total waste of your time. Go away and leave me alone or you will be a common criminal because violation of a restraining order is against the law. I can't make myself any plainer than that."

She moved to get into the Lincoln and he took a step forward. Her arm moved back automatically in case she had to take a swing at him, but he didn't notice.

"I'm trying to resolve this amicably, Sherri. I have

a right to see the conditions in which my child and future wife are living, don't you think? I don't want this to turn into a court case, but if it does, I need to be prepared," he said smoothly, as though they were the best of friends.

Sherri had to exercise Herculean control to speak calmly and not knock him in the head with Sydney's duffel bag, which really didn't weigh enough to hurt him. Gritting her teeth, she said, "Trevor, this is getting more bizarre every time I see you. One minute you're trying to get me to marry you and the next minute you're making thinly veiled threats to take me to court about a child in whom you've never shown the least bit of interest. If it does turn into a court case, you won't have a leg on which to stand. Don't try to contact me again," she warned. "Anything you have to say to me you can say to my attorney."

Reaching into her purse, she handed him one of Royce's cards and was pleased to see his complexion turn ashen.

"How did you get him involved in our business? Where did you find him?"

"Why do you ask? Do you know him?" she asked blandly.

"He was a classmate of mine in law school. I wouldn't trust him if I were you," he mumbled.

"He seems perfectly trustworthy to me. And if I were you, I wouldn't be bothering me. Go away, Trevor. I have a busy day and you're holding me up. Goodbye."

This time she made it into the Lincoln. She buckled her seatbelt and locked the door as she pulled out of the driveway with haste. Her hands were trembling, and she had to take several deep breaths to calm down. He knew where they lived, he knew where she worked and God only knew what else Mother Stratton had clued him in on. Hell, he could've found it all on the internet for all she knew. She drove to Hightower AME Church as fast as she could without breaking any speed laws and took the bag into the daycare. It was naptime and she could see Sydney on her purple mat between her best pals. Sherri didn't realize she'd been holding her breath until a big puff of air escaped her lips, which had tightly compressed.

Mrs. Haithco, the director of the program, saw her looking in on the sleeping children and asked if anything was amiss.

"Not a thing, Mrs. Haithco. I had to bring Sydney's dance bag because this is the day for her lesson, that's all. We were moving so fast this morning that I forgot it."

"Dr. Sherri, with all you do it's not surprising that some little thing would slip your mind. You seem a little flustered, dear. Is there anything I can do?"

"No, not at all. But since I'm here, I would like to check the list of people I designated to pick Sydney up or drop her off, just to make sure it's up-to-date."

"I can email it to you and you can check it and if there are to be any changes, just stop by in the morn-

ing. You know that any changes have to be made in person by you only."

Sherri said that was fine and she left, her legs not as steady as she would have liked. When she got to her office she apologized to Kayla for being late; being tardy wasn't part of her makeup. She was always prompt and kept to her schedule because she didn't like her patients to have to wait. Luckily, her load was light this afternoon, and she still had twenty minutes before her first appointment. She called Royce Griffin and explained the unsettling visit from Trevor.

Royce was on it immediately. "We're going to have to take some steps right away because it sounds like he's moved into the stalking stage. Can I meet with you tonight, preferably at your place?"

"Of course," she replied. "Is it okay if a few of my friends are there also? They're very close to me and Sydney and they'll help in any way they can."

"Sure, no problem," he said. "Does eight sound good?"

"Sounds fine to me." She gave him her address.

"I know some people who live in the same complex and I have a GPS, so I should be fine. See you at eight."

Sherri felt more in control after talking to Royce. Her watch told her that she had a few more minutes before her appointment, so she called Lucas.

"If you're not busy tonight can you come over at seven? There're a few things we need to talk about."

"Of course, sweetheart. You don't even have to ask. Is everything okay with you?"

"It will be once I see you," she said in a subdued voice that he barely recognized.

"I'll be there," he promised.

When she hung up the phone she felt better. She went into her little bathroom to wash her hands and splash cold water on her face. She was dismayed to see her face looking pasty and strained and she patted her cheeks hard to bring some color back. Just a few more hours and everything would be right again. Just a few.

When Lucas got to Sherri's place everything looked perfectly normal. Sherri and Sydney were setting the table for dinner, and Sydney was singing happily. She stopped long enough to give Lucas her normal affectionate greeting of a big hug and a kiss on the cheek, but minutes later she was singing again. He tilted his head to listen because he couldn't believe her tune of choice.

"Is she singing 'Walk Like a Man'? Where'd she get that from?" he asked Sherri.

She grinned. "The *Jersey Boys* soundtrack. I think she has it memorized. Yes, my thoroughly modern child has fallen hard for Frankie Valli." She laughed. Her brief laughter died and her face turned serious.

She sent Sydney upstairs ostensibly to pick out an outfit for the next day, but as soon as the child was out of the room she took Lucas's hand and led him out on the deck. She quickly filled him in on the events of the

day, starting with her conference with Royce Griffin, then Trevor's appearance at her home, her call to Royce and his plan of coming over at eight to discuss a strategy for handling Barnes for the next few days.

Sherri might not have realized how furious Lucas was, but he was utilizing every bit of control that he had to keep from exploding in rage. Something had to be done about the man. The very thought that he not only knew where Sherri lived, but also that he'd come over to rub her nose in the information was galling to him. Lucas wasn't violent by nature, but he would have happily beaten the man to a paste. If he knew where Sherri lived and the hospital where she worked, he undoubtedly knew other things, like where Sydney went to daycare and where her dance classes were held.

He tried hard not to let Sherri know how much her news upset him, but it took every bit of the limited acting skill he had to keep her from seeing the anger simmering under the surface. He put his arms around her and held her close, so close that he could feel her heart beating faster than usual.

"It's going to fine, Sherri. I got this, remember?"

She nodded and held him even tighter, drawing his strength into her body. "Let's go eat so we'll be ready when Royce gets here," she said.

It wasn't a very filling meal for a man, which was fine by him because he had no appetite. But it was delicious by any standards. Sherri served the chicken salad he'd made the night before, along with sliced to-

matoes, a green salad and her special bean salad. And she'd made a stellar batch of biscuits. He'd never been particularly fond of five-bean salad, but Sherri's was delicious. She mixed red beans, baby lima beans, black beans, wax beans and green beans with chopped shallots, red and yellow peppers and celery. The vinaigrette had a unique piquant quality that made the dish stand out. He looked at her quizzically and asked what was different about her recipe.

"Oh, I use dilled green beans and I use the juice in the dressing, that's all. I've always liked bean salad so I played around with it until I found a really good variety of colors and flavors. Do you like it?"

"I love it. I've never been a big fan, but this I could eat every day."

"You should eat it a lot, Uncle Lucas. It has lots of protein and it's good for you," Sydney informed him.

"Thank you for looking out for my health, sweetie."

"You're very welcome," she said with a dimpled smile.

Lucas handled the table clearing and kitchen cleaning while Sherri took Sydney up to get her ready for bed. He took his time while he was handling the dishes because he was afraid he might break something; he was that angry. It was obvious that this Trevor dude was crazy as a damned road lizard and as far as he was concerned, he needed to be behind bars. Better yet, he needed to be under the building with the bars. It suddenly occurred to him that Alexis wouldn't appreciate

getting the news secondhand, so he reached for his cell phone to call her. While waiting for Alexis to answer her phone, the doorbell rang. When he opened the door, there she was with Jared.

He raised both his eyebrows in surprise and said, "I was just calling you," but he said it into the phone instead of directly to Alexis. When he realized his mistake he scowled and clicked the phone off, shoving it into his pocket.

Alexis looked at him with concern. "Are you okay, Lucas? You look a little stressed. What's wrong?"

Sherri came downstairs with Sydney, forestalling his need to answer. She was smiling, but it looked forced to anyone who knew her well, and these people knew her very well.

"Come on in," she invited. "Sit down, everyone, and I'll get you something to drink. Iced tea, lemonade, something stronger? Whatever you want, I probably have."

Now Alexis looked at Sherri with worry in her eyes. "Something is up and you're not telling me. What's going on?"

"Just give me about two minutes and you'll know. Please, just have a seat. Sydney wanted to come down to say good-night to everyone before she goes to bed."

Sydney was the only person behaving normally as she gave big kisses to Jared and Alexis, saving the biggest one for Lucas. Before she could get tucked in, however, the doorbell rang again. It was Royce.

"Hello, Royce. You're right on time. Just let me put Sydney to bed and I'll be right with you," Sherri ushered him in.

Sydney, never one to miss an opportunity to meet a good-looking fellow, introduced herself. She held out her hand and said, "Hello, I'm Sydney. What's your name?"

Obviously charmed by her winsome smile, her pink-striped pajamas and her pink robe, Royce smiled broadly as he shook her tiny hand. "I'm Royce Griffin. It's very nice to meet you."

"It's nice to meet you, too. I have to go to bed now. Good night, everybody!"

Alexis stopped Sherri from going upstairs. "I'll take care of her. You go handle your business and I'll be right back."

So Sherri was able to introduce Jared and Lucas to Royce. She sat on the love seat next to Lucas, while Royce took the big armchair.

He addressed his first remark to Sherri. "Is everyone up to speed on the situation?"

She shook her head. "Lucas is, but Jared and Alexis don't know everything yet. You can go ahead, and I'll fill them in later on whatever they don't pick up from your comments. Is that okay?"

"Works for me. First and foremost, I think that Trevor is in a fairly fragile mental state right now, so by no means does he need to be anywhere around you or Sydney. She's a little doll, by the way," he added with a

grin. "I know grown women who don't have that much poise." Sherri smiled her thanks.

Royce continued, "I'm going to be filing a restraining order against him first thing in the morning so if you see him or hear of him within one hundred feet of either of you we'll have a legal means to keep him away, so that's that."

Sherri made a sound of relief and Lucas gave her a squeeze with the arm that was around her shoulders.

"I used the words *fragile mental state* because of information I received this afternoon. As I told you, we were classmates and fraternity brothers. I've stayed close to my frat brothers. I made a few phone calls and I think I got to the root cause of him showing up in Columbia talking about marrying you. It all has to do with money."

Sherri protested, "But I don't have any money except for what I earn, and it's not like I'm rolling in the big bucks. I do okay, but I'm no Oprah or close to her in terms of money."

Royce smiled grimly. "It's not your money he's after, Sherri. It's the family money. His grandfather changed his will and instead of the lion's share going to the oldest son, which Trevor is, or even being divided evenly between his grandchildren, the old man has come up with a new plan. Whoever gets married and produces a child first gets to be CEO of Barnes Pharmaceuticals and gets the biggest piece of the inheritance pie. It's that simple. And stupid," he added.

"Seems like Grandpa Barnes is tired of his progeny acting like spoiled dilettantes and he wants them to settle down and act like responsible adults, which to his mind means marriage and family. There're four children and three of them are married but they prefer living the high life instead of popping out some babies. And Trevor is just buck wild. He's got women all over the place and no wife in sight. So Grandpa thinks that this is going to make them toe the line," Royce said dryly.

"Well, his siblings are back in L.A. humping like rabbits trying to produce an heir first. So Trevor gets this brilliant idea—he's going to marry you and bring Sydney home to the old man because that will make him first and he'll have it all without lifting a finger. See, no one knows about you and Sydney. Because you never asked him for anything, he never had to own up to the fact that he's a father and he's trying to use that to his advantage."

Alexis had returned to the living room by then, and the look on her face was priceless. "So why is he being so greedy? He's this big-time attorney, so why is he trying so hard to get the promise of an inheritance?"

Royce gave her a crooked grin and said, "Sherri hasn't had a chance to give you all the dirt. Trevor is not a practicing attorney. As I told her today, we went to law school together and he was at the bottom of our class. He has a law degree, but he hasn't managed to pass the bar yet. Right now he sells used luxury cars in Pomona and, as you can imagine, the market isn't too

good for them right now. Not only that, he's in debt up to the top of his head. He owes money to everybody, including the IRS and a couple of loan sharks. From what I can gather, he's in deep, deep financial trouble and he's grasping at any straw he can, which is why he suddenly showed up talking about marriage and family. He's a desperate man and judging by his actions today, a potentially dangerous one."

Jared spoke for the first time and he didn't sound happy. "What actions today? What did he do?"

Sherri took a deep breath and explained the situation as succinctly as possible. Jared's neck turned a deep red then spread to his face.

"Oh, hell no," he growled. "Do we need to go have a talk with him? Because he's gonna have to stay clear of Sherri and Sydney if he wants to live."

"The restraining order should be enough to keep him at bay," Royce said, "but I'd suggest that Sherri take extra precautions until he gets out of town. He's not in any position to try to get custody or visitation, but he's determined so I think that Sherri should consider getting an escort until this is over. He obviously knows your schedule and your locations, so just to be on the safe side, a bodyguard wouldn't be a bad idea."

Lucas spoke in a low, lethal voice. "She doesn't need one—she has me."

There was no doubt in anyone's mind that Lucas would protect her to the death, but Royce had one more suggestion. "If it's possible, I'd take Sydney out of day-

care for a few days. Is there somewhere else she can go, someplace that he wouldn't know about?"

Lucas spoke again. "Absolutely. My folks will be up here tomorrow to pick her up and take her to their place on Hilton Head Island. Not a problem."

Sherri looked at him in surprise while Royce nodded his approval.

"That's a great idea. My feeling is that Trevor's not going to be able to obey a restraining order, and he'll be in custody before long. It sounds cold, but it's probably the best thing for him. His family can cite extenuating circumstances and get him back to California for some much-needed treatment, and he might be able to salvage the rest of his life. In the meantime, I know it's probably going to be annoying, Sherri, but you don't need to go anywhere by yourself."

Lucas's eyes had darkened until they looked almost black instead of their normal green. "Don't worry. She won't."

Chapter 18

Sherri didn't know how to feel about Lucas's surge of protectiveness. On the one hand, she was grateful for his support, but on the other, she hated the feeling that she wasn't in control of her life anymore. But they both agreed that it was the best thing for Sydney to not be in the center of the Trevor's irrational behavior.

"Sweetheart, nobody thinks that you're not the best mother in the world," he told her. "But we all love you and Sydney and we want to make sure she's protected. It's just for a couple of days. She'll have the time of her life, and he won't be able to touch her," he said persuasively. "Don't you trust me?"

"Of course I do," Sherri said for what seemed like the tenth time. "I just hate to drag your parents into my

drama. And I feel like I should be the one to take care of this on my own."

They were in the living room, long after Royce had left. Alexis and Jared were still there, giving their support while Sherri packed Sydney's things. Jared had brought the bag downstairs and Alexis helped her get the clothing and other things together.

Finally Sherri took a deep breath and decided that it was for the best. "I just never thought it would come to this," she said, her voice full of emotion. "I've been living my life the best way I know how and now this."

Alexis sat down next to her on the sofa and took both her hands. "But you're not in this alone, Sherri. Lucas and Jared and their parents are gonna make sure that nothing happens to you or Sydney, and that's all that matters now. You've got us, sweetie, and that's better than letting that idiot Trevor have the upper hand, isn't it?"

"You're right," Sherri said, resolve coming back to her voice. "You're absolutely right and I can't thank you enough. You guys need to get some sleep. Go on home and I'll call you later, okay?"

Jared agreed. "It's definitely time for my bride to get some rest now that she's sleeping for two," he said with a sweet smile directed at Alexis.

It took a few seconds for his words to penetrate Sherri's angst. "Sleeping for two? Lexie, are you... You're having a baby!"

She and Alexis hugged each other tightly and tears of joy flowed.

"We had our first official appointment today." Alexis sniffled. "That's why we stopped by tonight. You're gonna be an auntie!"

So the night ended on a high note with laughter after all. After Jared took Alexis home to bed, Lucas and Sherri were alone in the living room.

"You should probably get to bed, too, babe."

"Just hold me for a while, okay?"

They lay down on the sofa and he pulled a throw over her body as he held her close. Even though she didn't think she'd be able to sleep, in minutes she'd drifted off. He held her like that for the rest of the night.

The next day, Sherri found that sending Sydney to Hilton Head wasn't as bad as she'd feared. The elder VanBurens came in the morning with Courtney and Gabriel to pick her up, and she was so excited at the unexpected treat that Sherri almost believed that it was simply a fun outing for her baby. Dr. and Mrs. Van-Buren were so glad to see the child and so supportive that her fears were allayed all over again. After hugs and kisses and lots of goodbyes, she was alone again with Lucas, but he kept her spirits up. He dropped her off at the office and gave her a sizzling kiss goodbye, reminding her that it would only be a couple of days to the weekend when they would join Sydney and have a great time.

Work was definitely what she needed to keep her mind occupied. It was a long, busy day and she was grateful because she only had time to think about her patients. When it was time to go home, Lucas was right there to pick her up and everything seemed normal, except that Sydney wouldn't be home that night. Lucas surprised her by taking her to the loft instead of the condo. He said he had a surprise for her and he hoped she'd like it.

When he opened the door to the apartment, she was stunned to see a big crate in the center of the room with two roly-poly puppies inside. Her eyes lit up with surprise, and she hurried over to take them out.

"Lucas, they're adorable!"

"They're Sydney's birthday present," he said with a smile. "I know you said you were waiting until you got a house, but they're so darned cute, I didn't want to pass on them. Think she'll like them even though they aren't Corgis?" They were seven-week-old West Highland White Terriers and they were fluffy white balls with bright eyes and happy smiles.

"She's going to love them—are you kidding? They're so adorable. She's going to go crazy for them." She sat on the floor and let them crawl all over her with yips of joy. She'd never seen anything so sweet in her life.

"Where'd you get them, Lucas?"

"One of the hostesses at Seven-Seventeen has a friend that breeds them and when she told me that they

were ready to be adopted I couldn't resist. I hope you don't mind having the puppies before the house."

"They're just perfect, Lucas. You're the sweetest man in the world. I love you so much," she said before pulling his head down for a kiss.

His face broke into a huge smile because it was the first time she'd said the words he'd wanted to hear for months. She played with the puppies while he watched her, pleased to see nothing but happiness on her face.

He had another surprise for her, too. He'd bought her an outfit to wear to work the next day so she wouldn't have to go home to a house without Sydney in it. Everything she needed from toothpaste to new underwear was waiting for her in the bedroom. He picked up the puppies and took her by the hand to show her. She was once again thrilled by his thoughtfulness.

"Lucas, I really don't know what I'd do without you." She sighed. "You're so wonderful to me and my baby. I can't imagine our lives without you."

"It's a good thing you won't have to, isn't it?" he answered.

Both puppies barked loudly as if to agree. Lucas laughed and said they must be hungry. "You're lucky your daddy is a gourmet chef, ladies. Let's go grill you a steak!"

Sherri protested at once, saying they needed puppy chow for their tender baby tummies, but Lucas teased her by saying he was going to make them rib eyes for

dinner. They laughed and teased each other so much
that she forgot why she was there, at least for the night.

After a night spent secure in Lucas's arms, Sherri
went to work feeling like her old self. She stayed busy
and focused until it was time to leave. Just before Lucas
arrived to take her home, she got an odd phone call from
Mrs. Haithco at the daycare center.

"Dr. Sherri, I feel like you need to know this. A man
called here yesterday trying to find out when Sydney
would be picked up. He was told that we don't give
out that information. Then he called again today and
was told the same thing. There was a strange man loi-
tering around the building and security asked him to
leave, but I thought you should be aware of it," she said.
Sherri could hear the concern in her voice and thanked
her for the call.

As she dialed Royce's number, Lucas came into her
office. She told him what had happened. Once Royce
was also informed, he said he'd notify the authorities;
they were all certain it had been Trevor behind the calls.
Sherri's stomach clenched in anxiety, but Lucas was
right there to reassure her.

"Sweetheart, it's handled so let's go home and feed
the babies, okay? Try not to get upset," he soothed her.

They were on their way to the car when her cell
phone beeped to signify a text message. She frowned
at the screen, not recognizing the number. It was a picture and for a long moment she didn't recognize what

it was. Then she saw it clearly—it was her mother with a look of utter terror on her face. The caption read, "Mother Stratton wants you home right away. We're waiting for you."

"Lucas, Trevor has my mother! We have to get over there right now!"

Lucas drove to her parents' house while he talked to Jared on the phone and Sherri called Royce. When they got to the house, she was horrified to see the flashing lights of police cars in the street and an ambulance in the driveway. Clutching at Lucas's arm she stifled a scream. She stumbled getting out of the Rover in her haste to find out what was going on.

Royce was already there and he caught her before he could fall. "It's okay, Sherri. Everyone is fine. I had an investigator watching their house and the daycare center because I was fairly sure that something might pop off. I also had the police on alert. My cousin works for the Columbia P.D. and I called in a few favors. There's been an unmarked car here since yesterday."

"What's the ambulance for?" she asked in a shaky voice.

Royce nodded toward the house. "Trevor went a little berserk when he couldn't find Sydney. His plan was to snatch her—or try to. Because she wasn't at the daycare, he came over here and your mother let him in because she didn't realize that he was nuts. He started out sane enough, but then he went ape-shit crazy, oh, excuse my language," Royce apologized. "He started getting loud

and hysterical and threatened her with a gun." Sherri gasped. "That's when he took the picture and texted it to you to get you over here.

"But your father saved the day. He came home unexpectedly and Trevor was doing so much ranting and raving that he didn't hear your father coming in the back door. Your dad didn't hesitate—he beamed Trevor with a Louisville Slugger and knocked him smooth out at the same time the police were coming in the front door. Your parents have had quite a day," he said in the understatement of the century.

Sherri ran inside to see about her parents while Lucas took his first look at the man who'd caused his woman so much pain. He was handcuffed and bleeding slightly from his head wound. Lucas's only regret was that he hadn't been the one to knock the man silly. Royce seemed to read his mind.

"Look, I know you want to protect your woman, but if you'd put your hands on him he'd be dead right now. Scuzzbucket though he is, you wouldn't want to be the one responsible for taking your new daughter's father out, right? I do appreciate the additional information you got from your friend, though. When your friend found out that Trevor also had a drug problem, it made it easier to get the restraining order and keep the police on a 24/7 alert. I didn't want to say this in front of Sherri, but you saved her mother's life today. Without that additional stuff on Barnes I wouldn't have had all this backup," he said as he shook Lucas's hand.

"Royce, I appreciate everything, man. Send the bill to me and if there's anything I can do for you anytime, let me know."

"Hey, an invitation to the wedding is all I require. I have a feeling it's gonna be the best party of the year," Royce said as he laughed.

Lucas went inside the Stratton house to find Sherri sitting on the sofa with her mother sobbing in her arms. "Sherri, I'm so sorry, so sorry! I had no idea that man was crazy—just none. I was so wrong about so many things," she wept. "I was so wrong."

Sherri had her arms around the older woman, patting her and saying comforting words. "It's okay, Mother. It's going to be okay. Shh, calm down, calm down," she said over and over.

After a while, with the application of cool cloths to her face and sips of water provided by her husband, Mrs. Stratton did calm down. Sherri sat between her parents, holding her mother's hand while talking to her father. "Are you sure you're okay, Father? Did the EMTs take your blood pressure while they were here? Do you need to lie down?"

"I'm fine, daughter. Maybe for the first time in years, I'm fine. There's nothing wrong here that we can't handle, your mother and me. What I want to know is—where is my grandbaby? That man was going to try to take her," he said with anger in his voice. "I wish I'd

hit him a few more times," he added. "Damned crazy bastard."

"Sydney is just fine. She's on Hilton Head with Lucas's parents having the time of her life. She's perfectly safe," Sherri assured her father.

Her mother piped up, "Who is Lucas?"

Sherri realized that her parents had never met the man she loved. She held out her hand to him, and he came close enough to the trio to take it. "This is Lucas VanBuren, Mother. He's very special to me."

Her mother blinked as she looked up at Lucas. "My goodness. We have a lot to catch up on, don't we?"

"Yes, Mother, I think we do."

Chapter 19

If anyone had told Sherri how they would be celebrating Sydney's birthday, she wouldn't have believed them. It was a huge celebration with so many people invited that they had to have it at Alexis's house because she had a large backyard. There were a group of Sydney's little friends, including Courtney and Gabriel, the Van-Burens and Grandmother Delilah, Aretha Sharp and Alexis's sisters, Alana and Ava. Even Royce was there, looking debonair as always. To Sherri's surprise, her parents were there, too, and they weren't being stand-offish and stiff. The whole Trevor debacle had given them an opportunity to start over as a married couple and as parents, and they were taking full advantage.

They laughed and conversed with everyone and were obviously having a great time.

Sydney was absolutely thrilled with her puppies. She named them Sugar and Sweetie, and they were equally happy with her, doing their best to lick her face off. They tumbled around the yard playing with Alexis's dogs. The sight of all of them chasing each other around barking with excitement was absolutely adorable. Sherri was so happy she thought her heart would burst. Lucas never left her side, not even to cook. He let Jared and his father handle the grill because he couldn't stop holding Sherri's hand and looking at her with eyes of love.

Every time they had a moment alone he was kissing her madly, and she would giggle like a teenager in love because that's what she felt like. She'd always been a happy person, happy with her daughter and her career, but now that she had Lucas in her life, she was truly filled with joy. He completed her in a way that no other man ever could and she loved him more than she could've imagined. She understood now why Alexis was so blissfully happy and at peace. She had watched her friend smiling as Jared rubbed her still-small baby bump. They looked so good together that Sherri had a moment of wondering if she'd get a chance to share that kind of emotion with Lucas.

A while later, Lucas and Jared had gone into the house and Alexis made her sit down with her on the love seat under the trees. "Come talk to me," she said. "I think you're having more fun than Sydney."

"I am," Sherri said happily. "This is the best birthday party ever, isn't it?"

Lucas and Jared came out on the patio and called for everyone's attention. "I have one more present for Sydney, the one she said she really, really wanted. And because she's in on the surprise, she's going to help me out a little."

Sydney ran to Jared and Lucas and stood there with a big smile on her face. His father turned up the music and the three of them began singing a number that needed no explanation—"Sherry" by Frankie Valli and the Four Seasons.

They had a whole routine worked out with a cute dance as they sang the words to the classic song. When they got to the chorus, Sydney ran over and grabbed her mother's hand to lead her up to Lucas. They finished the song and Lucas took both of her hands in his.

"Sherri, you and Sydney mean more to me than I can say. I love you both so much, and I want to spend the rest of my life taking care of you. Sydney told me on Mother's Day weekend that she wanted me to be her daddy and I'd like nothing more than to make her wish come true. I want to be your husband and be her daddy. So what do you say, Sherri baby? Will you be my wife?"

"Oh, yes, I will. I love you, Lucas, and I can't wait to be your wife."

They kissed each other to a chorus of barking from the dogs and applause from everyone else. Lucas picked

Sydney up and kissed her on one cheek while Sherri kissed the other. Then he slid a ring on Sherri's finger.

"Mommy, this is the best birthday I ever had in my life," she said happily. "Look at your ring, Mommy! Do you like it?"

Sherri took a good look at the astounding ring and tears of happiness started flowing. It was a five-carat princess-cut diamond surrounded by smaller stones set in platinum. Before she could say a word, Lucas kissed her again. It was the best day of her life since the day Sydney had been born seven years earlier. It was hard to imagine being any happier than she was at that moment.

But in a few months she was even more filled with joy because the Saturday before Christmas she and Lucas became man and wife. It was a huge celebration and a joyous one. The wedding party was big, consisting of Alexis and Emily as her maids of honor, Lucas's sisters, Tamara and Camilla, as bridesmaids along with Alana and Ava Sharp and, of course, Sydney and Courtney as the flower girls. Lucas had Damon and Jared as his best men, with Roland Casey, Todd Wainwright, Royce and Roland's brother Duncan as the groomsmen.

It was a romantic affair, but the most touching moment was when Lucas included Sydney in his vows to Sherri and presented her with a beautiful necklace that bore a small diamond in the center to signify his commitment to her. Everyone in the church was in tears at this point, especially Sherri's mother, who'd become

the most doting grandmother in the world since she had come so close to losing everything at the hands of Trevor Barnes.

It was hard to say who had the most fun at the reception. It was held at Seven-Seventeen, and it was all about the great food, the music provided by David VanBuren's jazz group and the dancing, which never seemed to stop.

Sherri was having another dance with Lucas before they left to go to their honeymoon suite. They planned to spend Christmas in Columbia and take a real honeymoon later, but they were going to have a few romantic nights before then. Lucas looked down at her and told her that Sydney had told him what she wanted for her birthday next year.

"Already? What could she possibly want after this year's celebration?" Sherri said with a smile.

"Twin brothers," he informed her and they both laughed.

"We'll have to see what we can do about that," she promised.

"I'll do my best if you will," he said before stealing another kiss from his bride.

* * * * *

REQUEST YOUR FREE BOOKS!

2 FREE NOVELS
PLUS 2 FREE GIFTS!

KIMANI™
ROMANCE

Love's ultimate destination!

YES! Please send me 2 FREE Kimani™ Romance novels and my 2 FREE gifts (gifts are worth about $10). After receiving them, if I don't wish to receive any more books, I can return the shipping statement marked "cancel." If I don't cancel, I will receive 4 brand-new novels every month and be billed just $4.94 per book in the U.S. or $5.49 per book in Canada. That's a savings of at least 21% off the cover price. It's quite a bargain! Shipping and handling is just 50¢ per book in the U.S. and 75¢ per book in Canada.* I understand that accepting the 2 free books and gifts places me under no obligation to buy anything. I can always return a shipment and cancel at any time. Even if I never buy another book, the two free books and gifts are mine to keep forever.

168/368 XDN FVUK

Name _____ (PLEASE PRINT) _____

Address _____ Apt. #

City _____ State/Prov. _____ Zip/Postal Code

Signature (if under 18, a parent or guardian must sign)

Mail to the Harlequin® Reader Service:
IN U.S.A.: P.O. Box 1867, Buffalo, NY 14240-1867
IN CANADA: P.O. Box 609, Fort Erie, Ontario L2A 5X3

Want to try two free books from another line?
Call 1-800-873-8635 or visit www.ReaderService.com.

* Terms and prices subject to change without notice. Prices do not include applicable taxes. Sales tax applicable in N.Y. Canadian residents will be charged applicable taxes. Offer not valid in Quebec. This offer is limited to one order per household. Not valid for current subscribers to Kimani Romance books. All orders subject to credit approval. Credit or debit balances in a customer's account(s) may be offset by any other outstanding balance owed by or to the customer. Please allow 4 to 6 weeks for delivery. Offer available while quantities last.

Your Privacy—The Harlequin® Reader Service is committed to protecting your privacy. Our Privacy Policy is available online at www.ReaderService.com or upon request from the Harlequin Reader Service.

We make a portion of our mailing list available to reputable third parties that offer products we believe may interest you. If you prefer that we not exchange your name with third parties, or if you wish to clarify or modify your communication preferences, please visit us at www.ReaderService.com/consumerchoice or write to us at Harlequin Reader Service Preference Service, P.O. Box 9062, Buffalo, NY 14269. Include your complete name and address.

KROM13